Rid June 18

Praise for SE Jakes's
Bound by Danger

"The slow build and gradual development of their love story was a rare treat in a genre full of Insta-Love and quick HEA's. Plus, as with S.E. Jakes' other books, the sex scenes are off the charts!"

~ *Reviews by Jessewave*

"Gritty and vulnerable at the same time, the author does an amazing job giving you a healthy dose of suspense and realism with her detailed plot. I was a fan with her first book in the series, *Bound by Honor*, and Ms. Jakes continues to thrill me with her brand of love, lust and heart stopping cloak and dagger by men who will risk it all."

~ *TwoLips Reviews*

"I fell in love with these two guys from the beginning."

~ *Joyfully Jay*

Look for these titles by
SE Jakes

Now Available:

Men of Honor

Bound by Honor

Bound by Law

Ties that Bind

Bound by Danger

Bound for Keeps

Bound by Danger

SE Jakes

SAMHAIN
PUBLISHING

Samhain Publishing, Ltd.
11821 Mason Montgomery Road, 4B
Cincinnati, OH 45249
www.samhainpublishing.com

Bound by Danger
Copyright © 2013 by SE Jakes
Print ISBN: 978-1-60928-934-8
Digital ISBN: 978-1-60928-834-1

Editing by Jennifer Miller
Cover by Angela Waters

First Samhain Publishing, Ltd. electronic publication: June 2012
First Samhain Publishing, Ltd. print publication: May 2013

Dedication

As always, for my readers—you guys are the best!

Prologue

The water rushed into the sea cave, pulled out just as quickly, thanks to the current of the rising tide.

Jace and Sawyer sat with their backs against the wall, watching and waiting.

Their mission along the Ivory Coast had gone goatfuck after they'd completed their main objective of recon. It would mean nothing if they couldn't get their intel back to their CO, and comms had been lost thanks to several storms and the area's constant fighting. After escaping the riots that had broken out twenty-four hours earlier, Jace and his SEAL teammate had headed for the LZ, but pickup was deterred thanks to the continued instability of the area. No one in the military wanted another Somalia, and the SEALs knew that lying low was their best bet.

Jace knew that leaving the safety of the cave right now meant certain death.

Staying here during the high tide also held the possibility of death, but the odds were certainly better.

The past several days had turned Jace into a betting man.

Neither he nor Sawyer was in a position of rest, although they sat to conserve their energy, knowing they might need to swim out to their possible deaths, let the tide take them into the warm and shark-laden waters with strong currents and no safe outlet to swim to shore.

During their days in hiding, which had started before the cave incident, both men had remained quiet out of necessity, planning escape routes and other emergency procedures. Staying sharp, staying on mission point. But another part of Jace's brain had been actively assessing his life. Couldn't be helped, and he assumed Sawyer was doing a similar mental exercise.

At least thinking about Tomcat was keeping him warm. He'd met the man a month ago, hadn't spoken to him for all that long, but long enough to provide fodder for plenty of fantasies.

Jace had lived through much of his bucket list. Being with the teams meant he was strong, sharp and brave, and that wasn't bragging—it simply was. Without those qualities, he never would've made it this far. For most of his life, he hadn't let anyone or anything hold him back—he did what he wanted when he wanted in his personal life and served his country well.

The only risk he'd refused to take had been approaching Tomcat for more than talking. He hadn't been a hundred percent sure the guy was gay or bi, but he was sure that he wanted the tough-talking MC enforcer who'd been on scene with the Killers for the past few years. Jace himself had started riding with the group fairly recently, and only to help his cousin Kenny, who'd gotten way too involved with them for Jace's comfort.

Tomcat was the first guy Jace had really wanted. He'd been with lots of women, and he'd experimented with his bisexuality here and there before the military. But since then, he'd concentrated on the release adrenaline rushes gave him more than on orgasms.

Not that he'd been a monk, but it had been different, more

of the wham-bam-thank-you-ma'am mentality. No one had ever hit him hard enough that he'd actively thought of them in this kind of life-flashing-before-his-eyes situation.

Now, he looked at Sawyer. "Think it's coming much higher?"

"Yes."

"How close?"

"It's going to reach us—just have to hope we can withstand the current and hang on." Sawyer motioned to a few rocks jutting out overhead. "We'll have to brace ourselves against those."

Jace looked up at them and wondered if it was really going to come down to praying.

"God, this sucks," Sawyer said. "I hate sitting around."

Only Sawyer would consider this sitting around. Jace was surprised the man had held out this long. Although the men looked similar, their personalities were pretty different. Jace was way more brooding, whereas Sawyer was happy to chat, to share. At first it drove Jace crazy, but he'd grown to accept it more over the past year they'd worked together. He grudgingly realized that having a friend like that was good for him, and he knew they'd both had the same requisite shitty backgrounds that seemed almost necessary to grow balls big enough to handle this job.

"Hey, what have you been thinking about?" Sawyer asked.

"Sex."

Sawyer laughed, the laugh of a man who'd been caught thinking about the same thing. "Keeps you warm."

"Yeah." Jace tucked his hands under his arms, watched the foam come closer before receding. "When we get out of here, I've got shit to do."

"Like what?"

"Tell someone I want to fuck them and hope they reciprocate," he said bluntly.

"Specific person in mind, or are you just going to walk up to the first person you see and proposition that?"

Jace smiled. "I've got someone in mind."

"Sounds like a big deal."

Jace wondered if Sawyer would care about the bi thing and decided he wouldn't. "It's another guy."

Sawyer blinked. "Oh. Does he know?"

"No clue if he does. But I've never, you know—"

"Me neither."

Jace looked at him in surprise. "Anything you want to share?"

"Not particularly, but hell, if I don't tell someone I'll never move forward," he confessed. "It's, ah, someone you know. But not you."

Jace laughed. He'd started to shiver earlier, and he wondered if they were both in the throes of some crazy, hypothermia-induced state.

Based on what Sawyer had just told him, things began to click into place. Because he'd had the feeling that his new CO had a thing for Sawyer. "It's Rex, right?"

"Ah fuck, is it that obvious?"

"Not from your end."

"Are you sure he's gay?"

"As gay as DADT—repealed or not—lets him be. Doesn't flaunt it but it's not a secret," Jace explained. "Does that change anything?"

"You mean, does it make me less of a pussy? No," Sawyer

admitted. "When did you know?"

"That I was bi? Maybe ten years ago." Jace shrugged. "I never really had the motivation to do much more about it than mess around, but this thing with Tomcat...it's killing me."

"He's one of the MC club guys?"

"I think he's undercover CIA, actually," Jace said.

"Are you doing shit that's going to fuck up your career?"

"Nice of you to care, but no. It's weird, but I get the feeling he's looking out for me."

They hung on until the fighting subsided and the tides shifted in their favor. By then, their arms were exhausted and shaking from holding on, their nails bloody and their voices raw from talking loudly over the water. Because if they kept talking, kept admitting shit, it would be all right.

They talked about the kind of crap you only say when your life is practically flashing before your eyes even as you try to pretend you're going to be fine.

Finally, the water pulled back out as darkness descended, and Jace had never been more grateful for the moon in his life. Now it was like a morning after, except Jace knew Sawyer would keep his secrets. He also knew the man a lot better than he'd ever known any friend and vice versa...and for once, it felt right.

"We're keeping those promises," Sawyer told him, a hand outstretched, and Jace shook it firmly.

"Yes."

They left the cave and climbed down the slick rocks, then waded through the low tide and walked along the beach to the LZ, with Jace more determined than ever to find a way to share his feelings.

Chapter One

Two months later

The party was in full swing when Jace arrived. Two weeks back from his last mission and the bruises and other obvious trauma were fading, but his resolve wasn't.

"Jace!" Kenny gave him a drunken hug when he walked into the bar owned and operated by the Killers, an MC gang with the reputation of being one of the most notorious and the most private. You could join by invitation only, and there was only a symbol on the rockers the members wore, rather than the actual name of their MC club.

Jace was an honorary member, his cousin full-fledged, which was the reason for Jace joining the MC in any way, shape or form. Kenny had gotten a couple more tattoos, including one on the front of his neck, which meant a respectable job was becoming more and more out of the question. "Nice ink."

"Nacho did it. Said he'd train me."

The tattoo parlor was another front the club used, and Jace was pretty sure he knew what Kenny would be trained in, and it wouldn't be learning to ink someone up. "I thought you were still doing construction?"

"Business is slow. I don't get called that much."

Because Kenny partied too hard and couldn't always wake

up in time for work. But Kenny smiled and said, "Come have a drink," and Jace knew this wasn't the time or the place to continue pushing his cousin.

He looked past Kenny's shoulder, and his eyes met Tomcat's across the bar, and Jace swore the man looked at him like he wanted to fuck him.

Or maybe it was wishful thinking. Then again, his instincts had been on target with the few men he'd fucked around with.

The day he couldn't trust his own gut was the day he needed to quit the teams, and today wasn't that day.

The woman who usually hung with Tomcat wasn't there, although some of the younger women were taking advantage of that fact and were all over the enforcer. One was on Jace, too, eager to help a young man back from battle.

Yeah, that's what the woman hanging on him said, and while he got the romanticized version some people had, he was also uncomfortable talking about it, especially with civilians.

So he brushed her off, had a shot with Kenny and felt Tomcat's eyes on him.

But the dark-haired young woman who'd eyed him since he joined was persistent. He'd managed to avoid her thus far, but she was going out of her way not to be missed tonight. She was slurring to the point of unattractiveness, so he extricated himself, assuming no one would miss him as the party continued to go full swing, and headed out toward the garage behind the bar, where the men shot the shit and worked on their bikes.

The last time Jace had been out here fixing his Harley, Tomcat was hanging around under the guise of helping. He'd asked Jace about his current status on the teams, and Jace remembered the concern on the enforcer's face.

"Cools said you were Army," Jace had said casually.

Tomcat nodded, and Jace continued, "Let me guess—motorpool? Or clerk?" Both were milspeak for Delta Force.

Tomcat snorted, neither confirmed nor denied.

Now, Jace hoped Tomcat would follow him out to continue their talk, and he wasn't disappointed.

He looked up from where he'd been rifling through the toolbox. The man was taller by several inches, and Jace was six foot one himself. Tomcat wore a leather jacket over worn black jeans, and his boots were heavy and steel-toed. His hair was long, pulled back in a ponytail, and he'd shaved his normally heavy beard into a more manageable goatee that he rubbed constantly with his fingers like he wasn't used to it. It still hid a lot of his face, and Jace wished the man would shave it so he could see the lines of Tomcat's jaw.

God, you're like a lovesick girl.

Jace tore his gaze away and focused on the bike—it needed an overhaul, but he'd have to settle for a quick tune-up tonight. While he worked, Tomcat began handing him tools, and then they were talking with an easiness Jace appreciated.

There weren't questions about his bruises or his mental state. They talked about the goings-on inside the club and the party, and then things changed when his hand covered Tomcat's instead of the wrench he'd been going for. It had been an innocent mistake, because Jace had reached back without looking, but Tomcat yanked his hand back like he'd touched fire before finally handing the tool to Jace.

He used it, then stood and threw it back into the toolbox, the feeling of Tomcat's hand still on his skin. "It's tough when it sits for months at a time."

Tomcat wasn't looking at the bike, but rather Jace's bruises, like he was cataloguing them. There was concern in his eyes, even as one of his hands rested on the seat of the bike, fisted, like he was stopping himself from reaching out to touch them.

Jace moved closer, wanting Tomcat to, but he backed away. The power of the chase rushed through Jace, because he knew the man was big and strong enough to take him down if necessary.

Tonight, he would push his luck. He had a promise to keep, and you couldn't cheat death and then blatantly break a promise.

"You trying to tell me something, kid?" Tomcat growled, probably figuring Jace would back away.

He didn't. "It's good spending time with you. Makes me feel...grounded."

Tomcat's stance softened. "The party too much for you?"

"Yeah. I thought it would be all right, but it's too soon," Jace told him, knowing Tomcat would get that. The return from any kind of combat was tough—for a while, Jace always felt like he was living in some kind of alternate universe.

Just then, the woman who'd been hanging off Jace pushed out the door and called to him. He turned to her even as Tomcat observed, "She seems like she'd be good stress relief."

Jace shook his head in the direction of the woman, who pouted and then disappeared, then told Tomcat, "Not my type."

"You don't like brunettes?"

He gave a quick glance to Tomcat's hair—Tomcat would've missed it if Jace wanted him to, but Jace didn't. "I like brunettes just fine."

Tomcat's mouth opened, then closed. Finally, he said, "Be careful what you wish for."

"Being careful all the time doesn't get you very far," Jace countered, his hand grasping one end of the handlebar.

"This club—me—all of it is playing with fire," Tomcat said.

"Did you come out here to lecture me?"

"No."

"Then why?"

"Tomcat—need to talk," Cools called then, before Tomcat could answer Jace. The man didn't glance back his way when he left, but somehow, Jace knew he'd won that round.

He also knew he needed to pretend he didn't notice what was going on around him, but he did. Tomcat was getting orders.

Enforcers in the club were a new entity. Usually rogue MC members, they were brought back specifically to deal with major trouble, and then they were expected to disappear.

If this was an undercover job for him, did Tomcat actually kill people in the name of the job? According to Kenny, Tomcat had been here for two years, back and forth, after a long period of being rogue—and in the Army—but fulltime for the past six months because of major club business.

That business—the gun-running portion of it—was already in the hands of the Feds—it hadn't taken much for Jace to uncover it. The MC trusted him way too much, or else they thought he was as stupid as Kenny. He'd never bothered to play it any differently, since being underestimated worked to his advantage in any and all situations.

In return, the Feds had given him some intel with the intention of helping to keep Kenny safe. Jace learned that a rival club was setting Cools up, and he knew that Tomcat could potentially be burned if involved.

Sometimes, fate was a bitch, but tonight she was Jace's bitch.

Chapter Two

Clint Sommers had left Jace and the MC party behind an hour earlier and now waited in the alley in Norfolk, wishing he was there for a blowjob instead of a meeting where someone would no doubt try to kill him. It was the nature of the job he was currently working, the nature of the CIA he'd been a part of for ten years since he'd left the military.

For this undercover op, he was called Tomcat and had referred to himself as that constantly so he wouldn't slip up and give his real name. He'd lived and breathed this character for years, and now he was an enforcer working for the Killers, a motorcycle club in league with the likes of the Hells Angels. Tonight, he'd been sent by his charter's president in order to make a trade with another charter—information he'd been told little about, beyond the fact that it was most important.

The alley was behind the bar the Killers owned and operated for the public. Their main clubhouse was two blocks down, so it wasn't unheard of for members to cut through here, but tonight it was deserted.

He was used to waiting in silence—his Delta Force days had trained him well. The CIA had honed his skills. The past two years working this MC gig had made him sharper. Angrier and lonelier, too, and that was getting harder to shove to the back of his mind.

It was technically still the DEA's mission, but they'd failed miserably at infiltrating the Killers. Under the blanket of Homeland Security, all the agencies were now actively working together, and so the DEA had borrowed one of the best agents the CIA had for undercover work.

Tomcat was flattered by that, but he knew the dangers involved better than any of them. And he would be simply grateful to get out of this one alive, although retiring Tomcat would be tough. That was an alias he'd cultivated for years, from when he was first enlisted in the Army.

Contrary to popular belief, the CIA did work inside US borders when necessary—and the American public was usually better off not knowing such things, although it seemed that everyone who'd never even come close to working with the CIA liked to voice their opinion on that matter. He'd like to tell them that not everything they read on the Internet was true.

So yes, his role as Tomcat had a long and storied history through the years; he'd earned himself quite a reputation. It was why he'd been accepted relatively easily into the Killers; his made-up background had him in the Army as well, which explained the long absences from the club over the many years Tomcat had been in existence.

The MCs had been started for men—and by men—who'd been in the military, warriors returning home from missions who didn't quite fit into their worlds. They were outsiders, and that was something Tomcat found quite attractive about the club.

But the violence for no reason, well, he couldn't stomach that. Too much stupidity in one place wasn't good for anyone.

Gun-running, he understood. Drug-running, no. He'd found his line a long time ago and wouldn't toe over it except in the name of the law.

And in the name of the law, he'd been waiting for an hour—too long. Something was off, but he couldn't act too sharp or they'd get suspicious. This MC didn't like smartasses, and they were always really goddamned suspicious. Even after all this time, some members would still accuse him of being a rat just because it suited their needs.

They'd be right, of course, but they'd never prove it. He was too goddamned good, although now he was getting screwed as he stood here, and definitely not in the good way.

Fuck. He hated being a pawn in their stupid war when lives were at stake because of their drug- and gun-running—and especially because of their connection to the Colombians.

That's what was important—not dealing with their ego wars. Tomcat was here for justice, but this job had gone on too long, weighed on him more than previous ones had. It made him wonder if it was actually this job or the combination of one too many jobs over the course of a lifetime of escaping death once too often. Everyone's luck ran out eventually, no matter how good or carefree you were.

He'd seen other undercover agents come and go, both within the Killers and in rival gangs, no doubt getting pulled off their jobs because they were taking up too much time and resources. Or maybe some burned out or had gotten killed—it was hard to keep track. All he knew was that right now, he was the only undercover who'd been buried this long on a full-time basis.

And he was stuck here. Dammit, working for himself was sounding better and better. Beyond this, he was worried about Styx and his situation—the man's father had escaped from prison and was causing a major problem for all of them. Tomcat was on call for his friend and partner whenever Styx needed him.

SE Jakes

Just then, a blond head flashed in his periphery. It was Jace, not bothering with stealth. The kid, who was twenty-five if he was a day, came right up to him with big brass ones and clamped a hand on his shoulder.

"Dude, what's up? Let's grab a beer." Jace's expression was innocent, his manner cocky, mainly because he could definitely back up what he was selling. Tomcat could only stare at him, his mind running all the possibilities and coming up with the only thing that mattered.

The kid walking into the middle of his job was no coincidence. Not after what had happened at the party tonight.

When Cools had called for him, Tomcat had never been more grateful in his life.

Truth be told, he didn't know what he would've said to Jace.

It might've been the truth—and that could've ruined everything.

It's good spending time with you. Makes me feel...grounded. Jace's mouth had quirked to the side as he'd spoken, his smile almost shy, and Tomcat's cock had surged. If he could've, he would've bent the boy over the bike and taken him, but this would never be the time and place.

Would it be, one day, when he was Clint again?

By then, it might be too late.

For Jace to admit that to a rough-riding, tough-talking enforcer took guts. Meant Jace was comfortable with who he was and what he did, and he liked being around others who understood.

He'd met the kid months earlier. Once the young SEAL had come into the picture, Tomcat at least had someone to actively fantasize about—and fantasize only, although before tonight

22

there had been times Tomcat swore the kid was giving him the once-over. And then he'd convinced himself that Jace was interested in his military background. Because Jace was active duty, too, and Tomcat had called in some favors to find out if the kid was also working undercover.

Jace had come back clean on that front, which didn't mean anything. But being an active-duty SEAL these days didn't leave time for much else, and black-ops jobs were a good way to get discharged. And after tonight's encounter with the kid, Tomcat had no doubt that Jace was at least bisexual.

Tomcat had to play this carefully, the way he'd been up until this point. Sex was a big part of the MC lifestyle, and thankfully, the CIA provided an agent who slipped in and out to pose as his old lady, because being gay or bi would not fly here. That way, he didn't have to worry about screwing women on the pool table and very few fucked with him. But he did get blown from time to time, because that was expected of him, and thanks to the size of his dick, he had developed quite the reputation. Legendary status, according to Cools, the charter president.

Inside, Tomcat was pretty sure he was dying. At least until this kid in particular had caught his eye and had given him something to look at.

"He's a SEAL—rides with us," one of the guys had said. "We gotta keep his nose clean, like they did with Jesse Ventura in the seventies."

Granted, he *could* be living out some idiotic Jesse Ventura fantasy. And Jace was a hero—but out here, it was Tomcat's gig, and he didn't work with any partner except Styx.

But that didn't stop Tomcat from getting hard every time he saw Jace. This time was no exception, but he willed his dick down, told Jace, "Get. The fuck. Out of here."

"No. Come on, man—let's go blow off some steam," Jace insisted, acting way too innocent not to know he was fucking things up.

So yeah, Jace and his not-so-innocent innocence had been a thorn in his side—and a jerk-off fantasy—for the past few months. Thankfully for Tomcat's sanity, the Navy called Jace back for missions more often than not, and more than once he'd thought about confessing his true profession in order to stop the boy from continuing to run with this dangerous crowd.

Jace's cousin Kenny was involved in the MC—Tomcat assumed that's why Jace was riding with them as well. He knew that other active-duty military had ridden with the Angels through the years—and the club had protected them and not gotten them involved in any illegal shit. It didn't mean the kid was bulletproof.

But hey, if the boy had a death wish—and Tomcat had little doubt that Jace did—that was his own problem.

Except that Jace was in the middle of a potential deadly one. And even though Tomcat had found himself relieved to see the boy when he'd come to the party, because it meant the kid had returned from his current mission in one piece, he was pissed at himself for even thinking about Jace and his cock when he should be covering his ass.

Tomcat sensed the danger rather than saw it, grabbed Jace and pushed him down. At least the kid had enough sense to stay there and not try to be a hero. Shots rang out seconds later above their heads, and both men cursed as the bullets pinged off the metal dumpsters and ricocheted by their heads, far too close for comfort. Tomcat pulled his gun and fired back to let whomever it was know they weren't going down without a fight.

But the shooting stopped. It had been a warning. Or maybe he'd been in the wrong place at the wrong time. Either way, it was time to get the hell out of this alley.

And he was way too aware of Jace's body under his. The boy's face was half-buried in his shoulder, and Tomcat leaned in and murmured, "Hey kid, do you see now that you're gonna get yourself in trouble if you keep hanging out with us?"

"Not a kid," was all Jace said.

Tomcat snorted. "Let's go."

He'd take the boy back to the safety of his place. The MC told Jace they would cover his ass in any way necessary, and taking him to safety constituted that in Tomcat's mind.

It would also give him time to interrogate the little shit and figure out how he knew what was really going down. If Jace was working against him or trying to undermine him, Tomcat would have to fix that. He would have to put the attraction aside to get to the bottom of things.

But he would get there.

He dragged the boy behind him, his gun down at his side until they reached his car. Safely inside, neither man said a word until Tomcat pulled in to the garage that attached to the building where his loft was.

His loft—the entire building, actually—was CIA-owned and had been a part of his long-assed cover. His loft was steel-reinforced, soundproofed, had bulletproof glass with blackout tint, and no one was allowed up here, not even the agent who played his old lady—for her safety. Still, it was furnished so anyone who visited wouldn't notice any of the high-tech gadgetry or the insulation.

He still checked for bugs daily and changed the alarm code every morning as well. Now, Jace came in behind him, and Tomcat closed and locked the door, alarmed it and swept the room silently.

"Can't be too careful," he said, more to himself than to Jace when he was finished. Jace would think the paranoia normal for someone in the MC, especially a hired gun.

If he thought differently, it didn't show. He just nodded, at least until Tomcat slammed him against the wall, his gun pulled.

"You set me up?" he demanded.

"No." The kid barely blinked, even with Tomcat's elbow at his throat, gun to his head. "In case you didn't notice, I saved your ass."

The he leaned in and whispered, "UC. I'd say Fed, but I think you'd be offended."

Tomcat pressed the gun harder to Jace's temple, but still he continued, "Spook," with a warm puff of air against Tomcat's cheek. "I'm young, but I'm not dumb."

No, indeed; to be a special forces soldier, he wouldn't be. He could be as dangerous as Tomcat himself was, if not more so.

Well, fuck me.

"I know you need to deny it, but dude, come on," Jace said.

"Dude, you need to shut it." But Tomcat wanted more from him. The man was so close—they were both hard—and no, he definitely hadn't been wrong about Jace's wants.

"We clean in here?" Jace asked. "I saw you sweep, but I still need to know."

Tomcat ignored his question, said instead, "You fucked up my job." When Jace didn't answer, he admitted, "We're clean here."

"I was stopping you," Jace told him.

"Why? Trying to save my soul? Don't bother."

"From shooting Jerry's brother. It was a setup." Jace stared

at him with those goddamned deep blue eyes. What the hell—
had Tomcat gotten sloppy, or was the club being deliberately sly
because they'd stopped trusting him?

"How do you know this?" he demanded.

"I'm a little smarter than the average MC member."

What he meant was better trained, would notice far more
than the others. And Tomcat had no reason not to trust him.
"You're going to have to tell me everything you know."

Jace nodded, and he did, told him about the rival gang's—
and its president, Jerry's—issues. "It's not about you—Cools
trusts you. But he also knows that if you killed Jerry's brother,
Carl would be blamed, and it could start the internal war they
want. Cools wants a leg up on Jerry and Carl's territory."

Damn. Tomcat slid a hand through his hair and turned
away. He knew that the Killers fought with lesser gangs like
Carl's all the time, but he hadn't seen this shit coming.

"You're not telling them I ratted, are you?"

"Never."

"I'd trust you more if you were an MC member."

Tomcat wanted to be offended but couldn't. There was too
much truth in that statement. Finally, he put his gun away,
pocketed it but kept his arm on Jace's throat. Mainly because
he was enjoying the proximity, never mind that his entire job
could be blown to shit.

But this kid wouldn't turn him in. The consequences to his
career would be too great.

"We've got to lie low for the weekend, especially since we're
already well into Saturday." Tomcat stared at him hard. "You're
sure no one saw you?"

"They know there's nothing I can do without putting my
military career on the line. No one fucks with me—no one

follows me."

Tomcat didn't know how completely true that was, but if what Jace had told him about the setup proved true, there were way too many people watching Tomcat's six. Hell, even one was too many. "You're going to have to drop out and figure out a story as to why we met up."

Jace shrugged. "Can't we just be hanging out? I mean, your background's military. They know that. Keeping the lie as simple as possible and as close to the truth usually works best."

Tomcat finally pushed away from him because he needed space. Needed to think. He poured himself a soda and chewed on some crushed ice as he mulled Jace's suggestion over. Could work, he supposed, but something nagged at him.

He didn't want anything about this mission to come back and haunt him. And Jace...hell, they'd killed men for less. "Why the hell did you think hanging out with this group would be such a good idea?"

Jace's jaw tightened—if he had an answer, he wasn't about to spill it. Not tonight, but Tomcat was confident he could get it out of him, so for the moment, he changed tactics. "You hungry?"

"Maybe."

Yeah, SEALs ate like teenage boys. He was pretty sure Jace was no exception. "Fridge is stocked. Make yourself comfortable. Oh, and give me your phone."

"Fuck that." He brushed past Tomcat. "Make me."

Oh, this boy was going down. Would lie writhing and begging under him by the time all was said and done.

It was like Jace knew it, too, and was taking advantage as much as possible before that happened. And after the boy downed a sandwich or two and a soda, Tomcat asked, "So the only reason you found me was to warn me?"

"Yes." Jace flicked his gaze coolly over him.

"I don't think so." Tomcat was done forcing himself to believe it was nothing more than a natural suspicion—he knew better. "No one knows I live here. No one knows you're here. Do you understand how much trouble you could be in?"

Jace moved from the table over to where Tomcat was pacing. He slid his body in between Tomcat's and the wall and breathed, "Yeah. Go ahead and punish me."

There were inches separating them, and Tomcat liked to pretend he was made of steel—and most of the time it worked—but the proximity was too much. Jace might've been teasing, but Tomcat would up the ante, take it to the next level and see what the boy would do then.

The boy. An intimate term he'd never thought he'd use on anyone again. This night was turning out to be full of surprises.

"Son of a bitch," Tomcat muttered before bringing his mouth down on Jace's. This was the moment—he'd been waiting for it for a while now, and he drank the boy in until both were nearly breathless. Tomcat didn't want to stop, and obviously Jace didn't want him to. The boy had gripped the waist of his leather pants and was holding their pelvises together, crotches rubbing, and Jesus, this was as hot as anything.

"Fuck me now." Jace whispered his demands when Tomcat pulled back, and it took everything he had not to rip the boy's clothes off immediately and follow his orders. Instead, he bent and kissed Jace again until he figured out the best course of action.

Jace couldn't decide if this was the best thing he'd ever

done or the stupidest, figured it was a draw and tried not to let his nerves show as Tomcat's kisses became more demanding. And fuck it all, he really liked it, as he knew he would.

But just when he was ready to take off all his damned clothes, Tomcat's phone rang, and he pulled away, grumbled and took the call while Jace watched him, trying to pull himself together.

Jace had known he was bisexual for a long time but hadn't done more than kiss and get blowjobs from random men throughout the years. Once in the military, the guy-on-guy thing became harder, and instead of finding his satisfaction with women, he went into the fantasy-and-his-own-hand route for satisfaction. And that worked for a little while.

When his fantasies had gotten too big and insistent enough to pull him away from movies and his hand, he'd done some investigating and discovered this club that specialized in making fantasies come true. They linked Doms with one-time subs—all free and on the up-and-up—and everyone was screened for safety. And privacy. But he'd quickly realized that going out and cruising gay clubs in the area wasn't an option now—he was too new and inexperienced, never mind active-duty military. And he really didn't know if this was something best kept a fantasy.

But judging by how hard his dick was, *this* was exactly what he wanted, and he didn't have to go to that club to find out.

No, he'd pretty much known it the minute he'd laid eyes Tomcat in the clubhouse bar. Jace had gone home that night and had his first wet dream since he was a preteen.

When he'd caught wind of the way things were going down at the MC tonight, he knew from the first that the former military man could be in trouble, and something in Jace's gut told him the man was undercover. Maybe because he was as well, but for the FBI, not CIA. Tomcat wasn't a Fed, and the man would be pissed as hell if he thought Jace was horning in on his territory. Being a part of this MC in any way, shape or form was practically a suicide attempt anyway.

He had the perfect in with his cousin Kenny, who'd always been too fucking dimwitted for his own good. The fact that Jace was active duty gave this chapter bragging rights. And the FBI had been counting on that, needed intel on the drug ring.

Jace's motives had been selfish—the only way his cousin could leave the club was literally by dying. If Jace did his job right, Kenny would get witness protection. It wasn't optimal, but otherwise the man would end up six feet under.

But now, Kenny and the MC and the Feds were the furthest thing from his mind, especially when Tomcat hung the phone up and, without a moment's hesitation, grabbed him. Jace waited for him to kiss him, strip him, to do something, because his body was practically vibrating with need.

Tomcat just watched him for a long second, like he was reading his mind, then brushed a hand over Jace's cheek. "You've done this before, right?" he asked as Jace tried to breathe. He managed to shake his head and wondered how much of a problem it was going to be for Tomcat. Because Jace refused to let it be any kind of problem for him.

"So exactly how much of a virgin are you?" Tomcat continued.

Jace gave him the cocked-eyebrow, self-assured look that told him he wasn't worried that he'd never been with a guy for actual sex, even though the reality was that he was nervous as hell. "Enough of one. Why, you into that?"

"Yeah, I am, actually."

Jace jolted as Tomcat's hand cupped his cock, a hard

finger pressed under his balls. "*Really* into that. Because there's nothing like watching a virgin get fucked for the first time, and I like being the one doing the fucking."

A sudden image of him pinned beneath Tomcat, spread and begging, made his dick leak. He might've shuddered a little as a contraction of pleasure shot through him, and Tomcat smirked—the look of a predator who knew he had his prey just where he wanted it.

"So what are you waiting for, then?" Jace managed anyway.

"I want you—trust me. But it's not going to be painless."

"Do I look like I have trouble handling a little pain?" Jace couldn't help it—he reached for the man's zipper, found that Tomcat liked to go commando. He pulled away to look down at the long, hard dick he'd started to stroke. And then slowly, he sank to his knees, because all he wanted to do was taste this man.

Tomcat grabbed his shoulders and attempted to draw him up, saying, "I *have* done this before, so why don't you let me lead?"

But Jace couldn't. Not yet. "Don't stop me. Jesus, please don't," he heard himself murmur—hell, maybe he was even begging—and then Tomcat let out a rough groan and surrendered to Jace's touch. His hand circled the hard cock; his mouth sought to taste the salty precome already leaking.

He closed his eyes and let his natural instincts take over. Held Tomcat's hips and let the man wind a hand in his hair and lead him along as he took Tomcat's cock as deeply as he could into his mouth.

He could immediately see why a guy doing this to another guy could make it so much better. Jace just knew the right places to lick, the right amount of pressure to apply, the way to use his teeth for pleasure and not pain. He liked the taste of

Tomcat's dick in his mouth, the feel of his heavy balls in his hand. He sucked up and down, worked his tongue in and out of Tomcat's pisshole, and when he heard Tomcat's stuttered moan, he figured he was doing things right. He was enjoying the hell out of it on his end. When he looked up and met Tomcat's eyes, he was close to losing it in his pants. Obviously, the man felt the same way, because he tried to pull Jace away from him.

But Jace was having none of that, wanted the satisfaction of making the more experienced man come first.

When Jace refused to move, Tomcat stopped giving him the option and shot down his throat, and Jace swallowed the hot, salty liquid even as his own orgasm overtook him, shaking him to the core.

Despite that, he was still hard.

Tomcat knew he'd remember the way Jace stared up at him every time he found himself on the receiving end of a blowjob. The boy's eyes were fierce with intent, his mouth wrapped around Tomcat's cock, and the vibration from Jace's moans ultimately pulled Tomcat's climax from him when that hadn't been his intention. Not then, anyway. He did plan on coming a lot tonight. All weekend, in fact.

Jace didn't ask if what he'd done was okay, but the question was in his eyes and the dark flush of his cheeks. Tomcat brought him to his feet and kissed him again, tasting himself. Letting Jace know it had been fucking awesome.

"My turn," he murmured as he touched the boy's slightly swollen lips. Jace didn't argue this time, but his mouth dipped to kiss Tomcat's shoulder. This boy was the best combination— tough as nails but still so damned sweet.

He would take his time here. "You're sure about this?" he asked. "We don't have to—"

"We do. Fuck, Tomcat...ever since I saw you for the first time, I've wanted this. I came to the alley to save you tonight. I didn't know we'd end up like this but I'm not sorry."

Tomcat wasn't either—now it was all moth to a flame, and it was dangerous to play with this fire. Because it was so goddamned right. This was a collision course he probably couldn't have stopped if he tried. And, to be fair, he didn't try very hard at all, although he knew there would be consequences later.

As Tomcat wrapped his rough-skinned palm against the swell of Jace's cock, the boy bathed Tomcat's throat in kisses. Tomcat inhaled the scent of Jace's skin as if that would allow him to track the boy in the future.

You could stop now.

But what would that change? Things had gone officially off the rails, and Jace couldn't leave now anyway. Motives had been revealed, masks stripped, and Tomcat was relieved as shit and too far gone to panic about it yet.

Jace nipped his earlobe like he was looking for more attention, and he was about to get it. Tomcat's moan in response was deep. Guttural. It seemed to excite Jace more as Tomcat pressed against him. He eased Jace's jeans down—the boy wore no underwear, which Tomcat liked. He circled the boy's cock immediately, felt the hot swell in his palm, heard the short, uneven gasps. Jace's pulse jumped—it was obvious the boy was nervous but too turned on to stop.

"Get rid of your pants," he murmured, and Jace complied as he sucked a hickey onto Tomcat's chest as if marking him.

I'll mark you, too, little boy—just you wait.

Jace's jeans dropped to the floor with a hard clank, his phone, wallet and God knew what kind of weapons hitting the wood planks. He seemed intoxicated by Tomcat's touches...by what he knew would happen.

"Virgin," Tomcat murmured, enjoying the tinge of pink on Jace's face. "Goddamn, this is going to be hot."

Despite having come earlier, Jace still wasn't going to last very long this time. Tomcat didn't want him to, needed to see the boy break apart under his touch.

"Come for me," he said, and with a few tugs, Jace did, a slow, almost torturous orgasm that Tomcat drew from him. His eyes only left the man's face briefly, and when they opened, there was a blissfulness to Jace's expression that made Tomcat want to roar with pride. Because it was only going to get better. He would make sure of it.

Chapter Three

Jace wasn't exactly sure how they got onto the bed, but they did, and he was stripped and Tomcat was halfway there until Jace tugged his pants all the way off. Then the bigger man hovered over him, staring at him appreciatively. He bent, tugged a nipple with his teeth, and Jace felt the sensation shoot straight through to his cock, despite the fact that he'd just come.

"Spread your legs," Tomcat told him, and although Jace was used to commands, he'd never really liked them...until now. Wanted more of them, more of everything. This was the relief he'd always needed, and had he known the roughness of sex with another man would be this good, he wouldn't have waited so long.

But maybe it was only this good because of the man currently fingering his ass. He jolted his thoughts back to the present, and Tomcat nodded as he slid one lubed finger inside Jace.

"Remember to breathe," he instructed, and Jace was ready to shoot back an insult until he realized he had been holding his breath. He drew in a deep one as Tomcat moved his finger in and out, tried to come to grips with the uncomfortable fullness. Forced himself to relax as he got used to the sensation and realized it was actually a good one.

And then Tomcat's finger brushed against something deep inside that made his entire body quiver and tense at once. It was a jolt he'd never felt before, and his cock was now impossibly hard. "More where that came from."

"Impatient, aren't we?" Tomcat teased, and didn't give him what he wanted. Instead, he added a second finger and then a third. Tomcat's machinations were slow, gentle almost, but it burned to the point of unpleasantness. "Push back against me."

Jace did and that helped. He was sweating, panting as if he'd just run a long damned race, and they hadn't even gotten out of the starting gate. He was beginning to really fucking hate being a virgin, because being new at something had never been any fun for him.

It must've shown in his eyes because Tomcat shook his head almost chidingly. Murmured, "Wait," and then his fingertips brushed that spot again, harder, without warning.

Jace's hips flew upward and his eyes rolled back in his head. He was pretty sure he shouted—curses, Tomcat's name— something as his hands scrabbled for the sheets and the undeniable intensity of pleasure filled him.

Tomcat did it over and over until Jace could barely hold it together. When he stopped for a second, Jace breathed and opened his eyes, desperate for more.

"Yeah, that's the spot. Remember, this makes it all worth it." He spread Jace's legs, and Jace hooked his feet around Tomcat's back as the man pulled his fingers away and started entering him with his thick cock.

The blunt tip penetrated easily, thanks to Tomcat's fingering, but it still gave Jace some pain. But he pushed back and urged Tomcat forward, wanting this part over with.

"Someday soon, you'll recognize that this part is also really damned good. The build-up, the pain makes the pleasure better," Tomcat told him, and Jace hadn't realized he'd said anything out loud.

It didn't matter—he was in good hands, the right hands, and he concentrated on getting Tomcat inside of him fully.

When Tomcat was buried, balls deep, he told Jace to breathe again. And then he pulled back and flexed his hips so he drove into Jace harder than before.

And Jace howled.

Everything was a blur after that.

It hurt, filled him until he was sure he would break, and then it was goddamned fucking curl-your-toes paradise. Tomcat nodded, because he knew, and Jace could only moan, because if he spoke, something completely unintelligible would come out.

"My sweet little virgin—say it for me—tell me you're my sweet little virgin." Tomcat's words weren't loud, but they were an undeniable command, and one Jace forced himself to respond to. Or tried to, anyway, forced out something that sounded reasonably similar to, "I'm your sweet little virgin," and it made Tomcat smile.

He wanted the man to smile like that at him forever.

"Doesn't matter how many times we do this—you'll always be my sweet little virgin, whether you like it or not."

"Like. It." His hips undulated, the pain transitioning, smoothing away to pure, unmitigated *fuck yeah* pleasure. "More. Come on—more."

Tomcat complied, and Jace gripped the big man's shoulders, refusing to let go, no matter how hard and rough the ride got. And it was gonna get rough as hell. It was sex at its most carnal, basic level. And it was exactly what he'd been looking for the past several years since the stirrings grew too strong to ignore.

The frenzy mounted—Tomcat's cock hitting his gland brought the pleasure to an almost unbearable level...and he became aware that he was yelling.

Good thing the room was soundproofed, or else everyone in the building would know exactly what was happening.

He was turning inside out. It couldn't have felt more right, couldn't be more right. And while Tomcat whispered sweet, rough, dirty things to him, he drifted off with the orgasm until his body was completely relaxed.

He wasn't sure how he ended up in the shower with Tomcat, who'd obviously dragged them both sleepily into the big walk-in enclosure with the jets spurting at them from all angles. He sagged against the bigger man as he was soaped up in all the right places, with Tomcat's thick fingers gently massaging his slightly sore ass, pinching his soapy nipples and sucking on his neck so hard Jace knew there would be marks. Wanted there to be.

"Mine," Tomcat whispered urgently, and Jace nodded. Agreed with a soft, "Yours," that seemed to please him.

There was nowhere to go afterward, and for once, Tomcat was glad he didn't have to do the *get the fuck out of my bed* dance. He didn't want to, either, and that was something he didn't want to think about too closely at the moment.

He'd cleaned Jace up in the shower. It had been hard not to fuck him again, but he knew the boy would be sore. Jace was also in that suspended state between sleep and reality, his eyes fogged, and Tomcat was content to lie there as they ate leftover Chinese and watched reruns of *The A-Team*.

Jace devoured the noodles as Tomcat knew he would. He made a call to order more. Jace nodded appreciatively, put the empty container on the nightstand and lay back for a second. "You've been on this job a long time. Kenny's been talking about you since he joined."

"I was there for his initiation," Tomcat confirmed, picturing the brutal ceremony that consisted of a brand that would remain on Kenny's skin for the rest of his life. Unless he betrayed the club, and then it would be mercilessly cut off. Tomcat had witnessed that happening, too, to others, could do nothing to stop it since it wasn't part of his job to stop men from joining this club.

"Two years undercover's a long damned time."

"It's not that bad," he lied.

"Bullshit." Jace gave him a small grin, the battle scars showing in his own eyes. Tomcat had seen some of the actual scars on the boy's body, planned to go over them again, for what reason he didn't know.

And the thing was, he didn't have to bullshit here with Jace. It was really goddamned nice. He let Jace run his fingers through his hair like the guy was freakin' babying him. And he let it happen, let Jace massage his back, feed him when the new batch of food came, until he was sure that two days would spoil him for life.

He didn't know if Jace was doing it purposely or not, but Tomcat pretended he was.

Jace knew. He hadn't been OUTCONUS for weeks, had dealt with almost dying, not by enemy fire but by water, and had gained a new respect for Mother Nature, so he was way calmer than Tomcat. The man was so tightly wound, Jace felt like he could come six times and still be clawing the ceiling.

And so as soon as he'd filled the man's belly, he got to work on the rest of his body. His ass was sore as anything, but he'd let Tomcat take him again.

He worked his way down Tomcat's chest as the big man allowed it, watched with that half smirk and the heavy-lidded eyes that Jace was beginning to love seeing.

He sucked the man's cock, felt the man's body tense and then heard the low moan escape. *Got you again.* Laved the head, tugged his balls as Tomcat shot into his mouth. Let the big man do the same to him, and before he could come, Tomcat was climbing on top of him. He stroked Jace's hard cock, held his legs open and commanded him to lie back and enjoy it.

"You have no choice," were his exact words, and Jace came in his hand when he spoke them.

"Baby boy likes that—takes his commands well," Tomcat crooned, and Jace wondered how he was hard again so soon after the earth-shattering orgasm. "But you're far from done."

"Good," was all he managed before Tomcat's cock drove into him hard and fast and took his goddamned breath away with every single stroke. His thighs were held apart, his head swam, and all he could do was keep his eyes open and watch Tomcat's face as the pleasurable assault continued, until he came in the fiercest orgasm yet. It left him weak as a newborn with what was probably an idiotic smile on his face.

And yet, as relaxed as he was, he couldn't help but wonder what would happen next.

Nothing good, he supposed. Especially because revealing his real reason for being involved with the Killers wasn't happening. Not with Kenny's life at risk. And even though he felt guilty about the intel he'd given the FBI a month before his near-deadly mission, he tempered that with the fact that he'd just saved Tomcat's life.

Jace knew where the Killers kept their gun stash—Nacho had been particularly mouthy one drunken night and let a few things slip. They were innocuous, or would've been to anyone but Jace. He'd laughed and drank and pretended he hadn't gained anything more than a hangover from that night, but in reality, it had been a big score for the FBI.

They were watching the two warehouses closely now, although they wouldn't move on the leads immediately but rather use them to try to hook some bigger fish, like the Colombians and whoever else the catch of the day was.

When Tomcat took several calls in a row and came back to bed even more tightly wound than before, Jace knew that when it was time for him to leave Tomcat's apartment, this part of the fantasy was over.

Chapter Four

Jace was sprawled out on his stomach, lying diagonally across the king-sized bed. Tomcat wasn't sure if he was truly sleeping or just so content he wasn't moving, but he kept an eye on him as he checked in with his handler.

It was Sunday morning—the weekend had blurred into nonstop sex and food, and Tomcat could think of nothing better.

"Get him out of there by morning," his handler told him. He'd been none too happy about the recent development, and he'd be even less so if he knew Jace had made Tomcat. As it was, he was simply pissed that Tomcat the MC enforcer had allowed someone in with the MC to get so close.

Yeah, well, that made two of them, he supposed. But it didn't stop him from strolling over and pulling the covers off the boy. Before Jace could even turn around, Tomcat was spreading his legs, mounting him, running his tongue down along Jace's spine and continuing along his crack.

Jace's breath caught hard, and he instinctively tried to move away. Tomcat anticipated that—the move actually worked in his favor. Jace's hips rose, giving Tomcat better access to what he wanted, and he held Jace's hips firmly and in place as his tongue circled Jace's now-exposed hole.

"Tomcat...Jesus..." Jace stopped speaking after that, when

SE Jakes

Tomcat's tongue speared inside of him, fucking him until the boy was pounding his fists in vain against the mattress, all the agonizing pleasure a good rimming was giving him pushing him over the edge.

He'd bet Jace was blushing—he'd waited until the boy felt a little more comfortable—and cocky—with the sex before he did this.

He buried his face inside of Jace's ass, not letting him go even after he came all over himself and the sheets, loving the way he tasted. He grabbed the muscled globes of Jace's ass hard, wanting to leave imprints of his hands there. Wanted the boy to have memories of this weekend forever.

And finally, when Jace collapsed, nearly wrung out, Tomcat flipped him and lubed him carefully. But Jace was so beyond fighting—was lying there open to anything Tomcat wanted to do to him, which made his cock even harder.

He entered the boy slowly, at first watching for any signs of discomfort as he fucked him more gently than he had since this started. When Jace was moaning enough for Tomcat to know there was no pain, he buried his face against the boy's neck, his hair, let the boy hold him as they both came in a shuddering rush, and he wondered what the fuck he'd been thinking, getting this close to someone.

An hour later he sat, showered and fully dressed, on the edge of the bed, while Jace lay there naked, taunting him.

He couldn't go there again, no matter how much he wanted to. Had to get Jace out of here and out of the MC, for both their sakes. The time for fun was over—the serious discussion needed to start. "You walked into the middle of something you weren't supposed to. You need to stop courting danger."

"I like riding," Jace told him.

"Find yourself another group. A legal one. Get your SEAL

buddies together. You're going to get yourself kicked out of the military—or worse."

"I'm not in the military because I like safe or easy," Jace pointed out as he got off the bed and tugged his jeans on.

"You can shower if you want," Tomcat offered, and Jace gave him a small smile.

"I want to smell you on me for a while."

Jesus Christ, he almost came in his pants. He looked away and heard Jace's laughter, even as he asked, "What happens now?"

"You go away on your mission, and you don't come back to the MC. Anyone questions you, say your CO threatened your ass," Tomcat said, knowing that wasn't the question Jace wanted answered at all.

"You trust me, right?"

Tomcat stared. "I don't trust anyone."

"That's great." Jace blew out a frustrated breath. "Well, you're welcome for saving your ass."

Tomcat nodded, opened his mouth to say something flip about Jace's ass but the look in the boy's eyes...

No, Tomcat could deny that something happened between them to everyone but himself. "You'll be safe if you stay away."

"What about you?"

He was about to say, "Don't worry about me," but instead he told the boy, "I'll be all right. If you wait half an hour, some agents will come by to make sure you get home safely."

"I don't need the CIA to escort me out," Jace said irritably. "Plus, then they'll have to know shit. Just tell them you figured it out. This way, you'll owe me."

"How do you plan on collecting?"

"More weekends like this one," Jace told him. Left out the side door and somehow disappeared like smoke down the fire escape into the early-morning darkness.

And the room was empty and cold again, the way it had been for years.

Chapter Five

Tomcat had spent his time shuffling back and forth between the MC gig and helping Styx with his problems, which included gunning down the man's father, a known assassin, right after Jace had left.

Styx and his old lover, Law, had been in witness protection with Law's current boyfriend, Paulo. And while they'd had their share of good sex, from what Styx told him, they'd also all fallen in love. With Tomcat's help, they'd gotten rid of Styx's father, and now Styx could live a life free of the CIA for the first time in nearly sixteen years.

So Styx was safe—and back with the old love of his life as well as a new one. Styx was the happiest Tomcat had ever seen him—and since he was happy, he decided Tomcat needed to be just as happy.

"He's too young," Tomcat told Styx on his cell now as he drove his truck to meet his Killers contact, wishing he'd never confided about Jace to him. A weak moment, a sappy-as-hell moment, actually, when he'd confessed how Jace made him feel...and more. Since then, Styx had been on him about it, wanting to know if he planned on seeing the boy when he returned from whatever far-flung place the SEALs had him in.

"Then why are you still in contact?" Styx asked.

"It's just texting."

Styx snorted, and Tomcat would've punched his friend had he been close. As it was, Tomcat's fists tightened on the steering wheel, and it had nothing to do with the fact that he was closing in on a hundred miles an hour. "I don't have time for this shit."

Literally. His handler had called him back to the MC because something big was going down—which meant the CIA and DEA's own something big would happen sooner rather than later.

"You have a right to be happy, Tomcat," Styx told him.

"Gee, that sounds familiar, you asshole." Something he'd been telling his partner for years while Styx wore a hair shirt for his first love.

"Yeah, well, it applies to you, too, if you let it." Styx paused. "I've seen the way you look when you talk about him. I don't think you realize it."

He realized it, all right—realized it was a big fucking problem. "Gotta go, man. Say hi to Law and Paulo."

He hung up without waiting for Styx's reply. Knew the man would understand, but he didn't have the time for this kind of shit.

He thought back to his early days in the service and then in the agency, and meeting James in the leather bar for the first time. That was when he discovered just how many spooks inhabited these places. In fact, he was pretty sure it was easier to be gay in his line of work, because there were no relationships. One-night stands, casual flings and no commitments were preferred.

James ended up working with him on some cases—years older and more experienced, having started in the CIA directly out of college, he led Tomcat through some of the trickier aspects of a spy's life. At the time, James had just met Glen, a young one who'd ended up being James's sub and companion for the next five years.

Tomcat really liked Glen, even though Glen and James weren't completely exclusive. He kept up with Glen after James had died—he'd promised his friend he would look after the young one, and he'd kept that promise. He'd just spoken with Glen yesterday.

The boy was finally happy again, able to throw off the heavy cloak of grief that had surrounded him for five years while he built his career as a Navy pilot with the SEALs, and all because of Derek, another Dom.

Tomcat figured that Jace and Glen probably knew each other and had no doubt done missions together, but figured it was safer not asking.

Tomcat had been a good Dom, but a twenty-four/seven lifestyle wasn't for him. He liked a submissive man, liked to provide the kind of stress relief a good Dom could, but he didn't consider himself a Dom any longer. Hadn't for years, had tried to explain it to Glen, who he knew needed the submission like he needed air.

But he did like virgins—he hadn't been lying to Jace about that. Taking that boy for the first time, well, there was nothing like it. Being the one who kept introducing him to new things, now that was something he'd yet to experience.

Jace had been willing to experiment—eager, always wanting more sex; he'd been the perfect weekend companion. And afterward, Tomcat never felt the urge to leave the bed, found excuses why it was better to lie there next to him or take the boy with him to the shower and then stay the night, if possible.

After another hour of driving, he pulled over in the lot behind the abandoned factory where he would meet his MC contact. But first he put his earpiece in and then pulled his phone out of his pocket and let his fingers linger on the keys for a minute too long.

Don't send it.

But he did, typed in the random check-in text and sent it. Immediately, his chest tightened. How he could miss someone so much was beyond him.

"We're on," his handler said in his ear as the MC guy called, "Hey, Tomcat, we gotta run," across the lot.

Tomcat pulled the earpiece out as he exited his truck, waved to the MC guy named Larry. He walked toward the car Larry waited next to, and in that split second, he glanced beyond the man's shoulder and knew something had changed. Why he hadn't been told about it was something he didn't have time to ponder. Instead, he kept his feet moving until the explosion shattered the quiet, and the last thing he heard was the ringing in his ears.

Chapter Six

They were taking fire from both sides, but Jace was too busy concentrating on the mission at hand, which was the rescue of two American Red Cross workers. Rex and Sawyer flanked him with a cover of flash-bang grenades and rapid fire as he worked to extricate the unconscious woman from her bonds. She'd been tied inside the abandoned building along with her coworker, who was barely awake and was helping Jace now.

Jace finally cut her free, and she fell back into her coworker's arms. He caught her before her head hit the ground, and then Jace took her in hand. "We're headed toward that Humvee."

"Through the street?" the man whispered over her head as Jace picked up and cradled the woman in his arms so if she woke, she wouldn't see what she was heading into. The guy wasn't that lucky.

"Yes. Keep your head down, your hand on my belt and stay close." Jace got a better grip on the woman and nodded to Rex. "We're going in three."

He counted down, and the man did as Jace asked, holding on and running for dear life. The trip probably seemed like it took forever, but it was under a minute from the time they left the building until they were inside the truck and semisafe.

The Humvee was bulletproof but not bombproof, and Sawyer drove like a bat out of hell to get them away from the line of fire as Jace worked on the woman and Rex readied to give cover while guiding Sawyer. Their CO was calm and cool under any pressure, and that made it easy for them to be the same way.

"Drink this." Sawyer pushed fresh water at the man, never taking his eyes off the road. "What's your name?"

"Hank. That's Lani."

"Hank, you'll be fine—so will Lani. We'll take you to an American base where doctors will look at you." Jace looked up. "If you want to go home, you'll be escorted from there."

Hank looked undecided, and Jace didn't blame him. Relief workers in this part of the world got the shit end of the stick—and most stuck with it despite the many risks.

He and Sawyer and Rex hadn't gotten called in to rescue these two. They were there on a much different mission when they stumbled on the hostages, literally. And they refused to leave them behind, even in the face of mounting danger. Rex had radioed to base camp that they'd found the missing Red Cross workers who'd been kidnapped days earlier and presumed dead even as he had Jace getting them ready for transport.

"We've got company," Rex said, quietly enough so Hank didn't notice. Sawyer sped up and took a hard right turn with all the grace he could in the big truck while Jace hung on and braced Lani, who was still out of it.

"Was she hit?" he asked Hank, mainly to distract him, since there was an obvious contusion on the side of her head.

"Twice, with the butt of a gun," Hank confirmed. "She started yelling at the kidnappers when they tried to drag her away from me. She went down and she's been out maybe the last four hours."

These two were lucky, although they probably didn't feel that way now. "She's breathing okay—pupils equal and reactive," Jace said.

"I tried to rouse her—she opened her eyes once, but she's disoriented."

"You a medic?"

"Yes," Hank said. "Lani's an RN. We came here together— same flight, although we didn't know each other before. We've been here three months."

"You'll have to give a full report once we're on base," Rex cut in, and Hank nodded at the big man with the big gun.

The ride would seem like forever—Jace knew from experience that just because they seemed like they were safe didn't mean shit. Too many things could go wrong, and he'd been planning for such eventualities since they got into the car.

He didn't doubt Sawyer and Rex were as well.

It took just under an hour before they reached the safety of the FOB, just in time, too, since smoke had started pouring out of the engine a mile back. Medics swooped in immediately to help the injured, and Jace brushed off the doc's offer to stitch his arm up for the moment.

"It's not that bad," Jace said.

"I'll give you fifteen minutes to get your ass inside to me," Doc called over his shoulder, and Jace nodded, although he had absolutely no intention of following that order.

He pulled his phone out and checked messages—it had been vibrating for the past several hours, but checking it had been the last thing on his mind.

The text wasn't from the number he'd been hoping to see, the way he'd seen nothing for the past month. Instead, it was from Kenny.

Shit. *Shit.* He closed his eyes briefly, then opened them and began to walk away.

Jace had been halfway to Afghanistan when he got the first text. Code, and he'd known exactly who it was from.

The texts, though they always seemed to come in at the right time, shorthand, were references to things that only Jace would know from their weekend together.

Those words warmed him when the cold, brutal nights had him hunkered down, waiting to make the kills he needed. It followed that way, a daily check-in for nearly five months, and then nothing.

He'd steeled himself for the worst and realized he'd found it.

"Hey, you all right?" Sawyer tugged his arm. "You just went white as a ghost."

He wasn't—and he couldn't just shrug it off. "Just some bad news from home."

Sawyer watched him carefully, his eyes narrowed with concern. "It's not...you know..."

Since their conversation in the caves, the men talked with each other about most things, from the banal to the serious. Sawyer knew that, while he had yet to follow through on his promise, Jace had. And now it was over before it had ever really started. "He's... They said it was a car bomb."

"Do you think it's true?" Sawyer asked him.

"I don't know what to believe. I haven't heard from him since right before it happened." Jace's inherent suspicion nagged at him, but either way, Tomcat could be lost to him forever.

"I'm sorry, man."

Jace nodded. "I'm gonna take a walk."

"I'll cover for you with Rex—and I'll take the first doc appointment."

"I owe you," Jace told him as he walked away toward a more secluded area of the FOB to try to collect himself. He knew Sawyer was concerned—once, that would've annoyed the hell out of him, but now he was all right with it.

It had taken him forever just to get friendly with one of the guys on his SEAL team—Sawyer had started to break down his walls with good conversation and an excellent aim with a firearm but sealed their friendship during their night in the cave.

Since then, the men had been as thick as thieves, with Jace trying to nudge Sawyer gently in the direction of Rex, Sawyer bucking back as hard as he could, and Jace...well...he'd thought he was finally moving forward, and now everything had come to a screeching stop.

Rex poured cool water over his shaved head and checked his team from a distance.

None of these men would ever admit how hurt or tired they were, and it was his job as CO to do it for them.

His gaze lingered on Sawyer longer than anyone else, the way it had since he'd taken command of this SEAL team. Watched Sawyer talk to Jace, and Rex realized that Jace looked pale as shit.

He'd wait for Jace to walk away before heading over to get the intel from Sawyer. The boy couldn't refuse him, even though he could refuse to admit why that was, and Rex wasn't in any position to push him. Not as his CO, for sure.

But man, if Sawyer finally made his move, Rex would have him pinned and naked in seconds. And after all the years of mourning a man he'd never had the real chance to say goodbye to, it was a relief to finally realize that he was ready to move on, that he could actually feel something for Sawyer without guilt or reservation.

He threw more cold water over his head when Jace left the immediate area, and he approached Sawyer as the doc put a bucket down in front of him. His SEAL's face was dusty but otherwise unmarked.

"Jace all right?" Rex asked.

"He got some bad news from home." Sawyer finished getting his boots off, sand pouring out of them. The sand didn't come off his feet as easily, and while Rex watched, he eased them into the bucket of water to soak off the dried blood and hissed at the burn of the salted water. "Motherfucker."

Rex shook his head. "What's the bad news?"

Sawyer glanced over his shoulder, the look on his face telling Rex he was breaking a confidence.

"I've got to know, Sawyer—I won't say anything to him if I think he'll be all right for the rest of the trip."

"He will be, Rex. Don't take this away from him now."

Rex crossed his arms and waited, and finally Sawyer spilled. "He's seeing some guy—CIA—and he got killed on an op."

"Name?"

Sawyer glanced up at his CO and something unreadable flitted across his face for the briefest of seconds. "I only know him as Tomcat."

"Get to the doc to bandage those feet. You're training today."

"Yes sir," Sawyer muttered under his breath, and Rex was pretty sure the boy cursed him as he went to walk away.

It only served to make him want the kid more. Dammit.

And then Sawyer called out to him, "You saved our ass today. Thanks," before Rex walked off, and Rex bit back a smart answer and simply nodded and accepted the compliment. He'd been at it a lot longer; his instincts were honed thanks to too many tragedies the rest of his young team hadn't seen yet.

Tomcat. Yeah, he knew that name, as he ran in those same rather small circles of elite operators they all leaned toward. Joint missions between the branches had happened long before the public knew about them, allowing connections between warriors who might've simply existed in a vacuum with no support. They'd also hung out after hours with other Doms they both knew, as they tended to run in the same circles as well.

He made a call to Damon, who'd be the one to give a message to a dead man. Damon picked up after several rings, and Rex said, "Tell your friend his boy just died a little with him."

"How did you hear?" Damon asked. They'd been friends for fifteen years—he wouldn't bother lying.

"Sawyer and Jace are good friends. And now Tomcat's going to let Jace swing in the wind?" He and Damon had spoken about Rex's attraction to Sawyer before. Actually, it was Damon who'd noticed it at a party and had been on Rex ever since to do something about it. Just because he was all happy and shit, everyone had to get matched up. Asshole.

"You're assuming too much," Damon said.

"I'm assuming this is a CIA stunt—and I'm betting Jace suspects the same."

"I'll tell you what Tomcat would say—don't say a fucking word, and Jace is better off without him."

"All you former Deltas are the same."

"Don't start with me, Mr. Unrequited Love." And then Damon's voice softened. "It's what we signed up for, Rex. Jace knew what—who—he was involved with."

"Maybe we need to treat our own a little better."

"Who are you really talking about?"

"Fuck you and that CIA fucker." Rex hung up on Damon, even though none of this was his fault. Being back here, in the field, was bringing back memories, none of them good.

In his new apartment that was an hour away from the MC club and ironically much closer to where Jace lived, Tomcat, the dead man, stared at the television and the Clint Eastwood Western marathon he'd been watching.

His old phone had been taken from him as evidence, but he still held the one he'd used with Jace. He'd thought about destroying it a million times a day, knew that he should and still couldn't bring himself to do it.

"You're supposed to be harder than this," he told himself. Typically he was a cold-hearted bastard, and that suited him. And this was make-or-break time for that persona.

He threw the phone across the room and watched it shatter into a million pieces.

It didn't matter—he knew Jace's number by heart.

Chapter Seven

Two months later, Jace still couldn't stop thinking about, dreaming about the entire weekend he'd had with Tomcat. There'd been nonstop sex, yes, and his ass had ached for a week after he'd left, but his heart had been filled with a strange sense of peace that remained until he'd gotten the news of Tomcat's murder at a time when he wasn't able to sit down and properly focus on it.

That the news had come from Kenny made it worse, since his cousin never really liked Tomcat much. And when Jace read the words, his first reaction was complete denial. He'd texted a few people he knew who knew people and determined that Kenny was right.

The president of the MC confirmed it by calling out a rival MC for the murder. And Jace could do nothing but shove it down, so damned deep he could no longer feel it, and continue his mission until he'd gotten all the tangos and had the okay to come home.

The coffin had already long gone into the ground, so now Jace stood in front of a shitty gravestone marked *Tomcat* and some bullshit dates Jace couldn't believe were real.

Rain poured down, which was good. Hid the tears that shouldn't be on his cheeks.

Barely knew the guy.

But even as the words echoed in his head, he knew it was a lie. He knew Tomcat better than he had anyone in forever—the connection had been there and damned memorable.

He hadn't been able to get more details from Kenny on Tomcat's death, just that the man's car blew, with him in it. And while that was enough to make Jace suspicious, the months of no contact were enough time to lay those suspicions to rest.

How he'd gotten so close to this man in one weekend, he'd never had time to parse. He'd gone straight from Tomcat's apartment to base and on a helo to Afghanistan.

Now he was home, and he felt like he'd lost everything.

Jace placed his challenge coin on top of the temporary marker and left, went home and drowned his sorrows and wasn't sure why the hell he felt shaken to the core.

He found messages on his home phone from some MC members—just a friendly head's up to lie low for a while. If Jace wanted, they'd let him walk away gracefully from the group—a military career could bring too much heat onto them once the top brass got involved.

Again, he cursed his cousin, wished the asshole hadn't been stupid enough to pledge his allegiance to one of the most dangerous gangs in history as he dialed Kenny's number.

"Hey, cuz, welcome home," Kenny said.

"You hanging in?"

"Yeah. Just doin' what you told me. Lost my job, though. The club wants to help me out."

Ah, fuck. "I'll lend you money. Don't take on any jobs for them."

"I already agreed."

"Dammit. What's the job?" Kenny paused, like he didn't

want to tell Jace. "Kenny, I'll come over there and strangle it out of you."

"It's nothing bad. I'm just going to be doing some pickups for Cools. They want me to start tomorrow night. I've got to go in for a debriefing tonight."

Pickups. Drugs, guns, it didn't matter. Kenny was one step closer to jail and/or death. "Didn't we talk about this?"

"I'm trying to do what you asked, but it's not easy, Jace. And you were away and I wasn't sure what to do." Kenny sounded frustrated and upset, and the guy was so stupid and young.

Several weeks after Tomcat's death, there had been a huge bust, centering around the warehouse Jace had pinpointed to the Feds months earlier. The Colombians were busted, along with one or two of the Killers, but for the most part, they'd escaped unscathed. According to Kenny, the MC was nervous from the fallout, and they started working at another warehouse with another group of Colombians. Jace knew the location but hesitated when he thought about telling the Feds any of this. Because, in the back of his mind, he was still tying that bust together with the work Tomcat had been doing. If there were undercovers involved in the new warehouse deal, Jace wasn't selling them out.

And still, he knew there was no real way for Kenny to say no to Cools at this point—he'd gotten himself patched in and tattooed, all before Jace had known. If he'd been home at the time, he might've nipped this whole damned thing in the bud. "Tell them you got a job. I'll cover for you."

Even as he spoke, Jace went to the computer and transferred money into Kenny's account.

"What kind of job?" Kenny asked.

"Fixing cars." Jace knew the local mechanic would throw

some work Kenny's way, especially if Jace told him Kenny would work for next to nothing.

"I'll try, but you know how they can be. And I think you're too hard on them sometimes—they've got my back."

Yeah, sure they did. And they'd stab him in it the first chance they got.

"Jace, Cools was telling me that you were close with Tomcat. Nacho saw you guys getting friendly."

Kenny sounded worried, and Jace sighed. "We had a CO in common on a joint mission. And we were hanging out at the MC when I was fixing my bike. Haven't seen him since the last party I was at—obviously."

"I told him that. Man, I can't believe Tomcat's dead."

"Yeah, me neither," he echoed. "What's the story?"

"Just what I told you—MC business. But Cools was concerned that maybe Tomcat let you in on shit that got him killed or something. He said that Tomcat never liked following the rules."

Yeah, that made two of them. "I don't know shit—Tomcat kept me shielded, just like Cools and the rest of them. Just tell Cools you got a damned job—I'll call you later." Jace hung up the phone and immediately called his FBI handler.

"I have to get Kenny out of town now," he told his handler, an agent named Mike McCall. "He's going to get himself in too deep."

"I need more intel," Mike told him. "We have a deal."

"Fuck your deal. Get Kenny out—I gave you the warehouse. My ass is on the line in more ways than one here, man. You've got to give me some help before I can't extract my cousin at all."

"I'll see what I can work out."

Jace didn't hold out much hope. Granted, he didn't have all

that much intel—and the sick part was, if Kenny took the job the Killers gave him, Jace could get all the intel he needed.

He paced the floor until he heard back that it was a no-go. Decided he'd have to do a little witness protection of his own at some point in the future, although he knew in his heart Kenny would refuse it.

Fuck.

When his phone rang again and he saw Kenny's number, he knew the shit was about to hit the fan.

"Jace, I told them, but they insisted that I work with them. They said it's time—that it would be an insult not to accept."

In this case, insult not so subtly equaled death. "Kenny, you have to leave town."

"I want to, but what the hell—where can I go? I'm part of the club."

"I know. But if you get involved in the job—"

"I don't have a way out. Look, you've tried to help me, and I've fucked up. I don't want to get you in trouble."

"You're not, Kenny. You just have to keep trusting me." Jace knew a couple of guys who ran black ops out of Omaha— they were always looking for someone innocuous to run errands, keep up the front. If he could put Kenny with them...

"I've got to go, Jace. One of the guys is picking me up in an hour and I've got to get ready."

Jace hung up before he could say another word and sagged under the weight of his responsibility. He threw his phone across the room, wondering if the helpless feelings would ever fucking go away. He'd had too much of them from childhood, and now they were returning with an unexpected vengeance.

SE Jakes

Jace put one foot in front of the other for the next couple of days. Went to base and worked himself out until he was too tired to do, feel and think about Tomcat, or Kenny and the fact that he'd gone on a goddamned drug run and was now in way over his head. He'd need to get Kenny a secure line or stop talking to him completely about getting out, because he was pretty sure the club was monitoring Kenny's every move.

Tonight, being tired wasn't working, wasn't enough to keep him from pacing his room in frustration. He showered again, letting the hot water sluice over his tense muscles, but he didn't even have the heart to jerk off. He bypassed the bed in favor of food and headed to the kitchen. He paused when he walked in that room because he swore something wasn't exactly right and then figured he was just too close to being out of combat. He was always suspicious and jumpy for weeks when he came home, and shooting at a random cabinet wasn't going to help him.

He leaned into the fridge and felt body heat behind him. Froze.

"I've died and risen before," the voice whispered, and Jace elbowed Tomcat—a very much alive Tomcat—in the ribs and pushed away.

"Goddamn it." He whirled around and stared at the man he'd been mourning. Deep down, he'd suspected as much but refused to let himself believe.

Dead or disappeared—either way, he'd assumed Tomcat was gone from his life forever. "You can't just show up like this, you asshole."

Tomcat shrugged unapologetically and Jace fought the urge to punch him as hard as he could. Tomcat didn't say anything, and he looked like a completely different person and still completely hot.

64

His hair was shorter but still pulled back, eyes were green, not brown, and his skin was smooth-shaven and tanned.

If anyone passed him on the street, they might see a slight resemblance, but as far as undercover disguises went, Jace had to admit that the guy was good.

"What the fuck are you doing here, anyway?" Jace demanded. "You're dead, remember? You're blowing your cover again."

"Thought you were okay with keeping my secret."

"I thought I'd be included on the whole dead secret," Jace shot back.

"You know what my job is. How else was I supposed to get away from them? And you know I couldn't tell you."

Jace's eyes hardened. "Fuck you."

"We had one weekend."

"Yeah? Then what the hell are you doing here?" Jace challenged.

Tomcat pulled the cemetery pictures out of his pocket and slammed them to the table. Jace looked at them with a shrug of indifference, although he winced internally at how fucking pathetic he looked.

The rain hadn't hid his tears well at all. "So I was mourning you."

"I popped your cherry—that's all."

"Again, so why are you here if it was just a fuck to you?"

Tomcat paused. "That's all it was to you, too. You'll see. Give it some time."

"Now you get to tell me how I feel? I might've been a virgin, but I've had relationships before," Jace told him.

"We don't have—"

65

"A relationship?" Jace finished for him. "Got it, loud and clear. Guess the texts were a figment of my imagination. Welcome back to the land of the living and get the hell out of my house."

Tomcat didn't say anything else except, "My name's Clint."

Jace blinked. "What?"

"My real name—Clint."

Jace muttered something, ran his hand through his hair. "Great. Clint, get the fuck out."

Clint wasn't going anywhere, especially since it was the first time in years he'd actually been able to think of himself *as* Clint for any significant length of time and not Tomcat. Talking wasn't going to solve this problem, and so he moved toward Jace even as the boy put his hands out to stop him. There was pain and anger and plenty of other things he didn't want to see reflected in Jace's eyes, and so he concentrated on getting Jace into his arms.

"I'm not kidding," Jace told him through gritted teeth as he moved out of reach. "Don't turn this into a goddamned fight."

But it already was.

He'd told himself he was only coming here to stop Jace from being upset and then he'd walk away. The second he saw the boy in person, he knew he'd been lying to himself.

Jace might've been younger and just as strong, but Clint had been at this game a lot longer. He let Jace fight against him while he used his hands to get at what he wanted.

When Clint touched him through his sweats, Jace froze and then moved to punch him. He avoided it and worked on pure adrenaline to get Jace pushed against the counter and subdued enough to yank his sweats down and palm his dick, because Jace could give him a run for his money in a true fight.

God, the boy looked so good—blond and tan, his blue eyes glowing against the golden hue—and even though Clint couldn't ignore the hurt in them, he knew he could fix it. Had to.

"Let me go," Jace bit out, but he'd stopped struggling, just stood still and silent except for the rough breaths that broke through. "Please...stop."

A plea, but he didn't really want Clint to do that. The Dom in him had been trained to know the subtle difference between a true request to stop and one like this, where Jace didn't want to cave this easily. Telling Clint to stop was his way of lying to himself that he was overpowered, and that was the only reason he was staying still and allowing the hand job.

Clint could deal with that. "I'm not stopping, baby."

"I'm not your baby."

"Right—you're my sweet little virgin," he said, and Jace choked back a whimper at the reminder and his cock grew harder, precome leaking, color rising in his face. Clint stroked the hard shaft, refusing to take his eyes from Jace's, needing to see the change from cold to hot desire.

It took several moments, but finally he got what he wanted. Jace's mouth parted slightly, his eyes glazed and his hips rocked to Clint's rhythm.

"You missed this."

"You missed this," Jace whispered back, his voice raw, and Clint had no choice but to nod his agreement. Jace relented further at that, so much so that Clint was able to let go of his grip on the boy's shoulder and sink to his knees to take Jace's cock into his mouth. But first he tongued the tip, sucking in the white pearl of precome as the boy moaned his appreciation.

Jace tasted so damned good. Clint had definitely missed

this, missed the kid, which was what bothered Clint the most of all this.

He'd missed *Jace*. Fuck.

He shoved the sweats all the way down, got one foot out completely. He felt Jace's tentative fingers in his hair as he licked the underside of Jace's cock, shoved the boy's legs open further with an impatience he hadn't realized was there. One hand fondled the boy's heavy balls as he took Jace's dick into his mouth, deep-throating it.

When he heard Jace murmur, *"Clint"*, he knew he just might be forgiven.

Chapter Eight

When Clint had moved in on him like a predator, Jace told himself he should get out of the way or punch the big man—anything to stop Clint from getting too close again. And he was way too close, but Jace had been unable to stop him.

He wanted to lie to himself and say that Clint overpowered him completely, but he couldn't. So he'd let Clint sink to his knees one last time, because the bastard owed him. And it was good—probably better than he'd remembered.

As Clint's mouth worked him, tongue and a light scrape of teeth—just enough to make Jace jolt with pleasure—Jace knew this man could easily get him back into bed. Maybe he was the biggest fucking fool alive for admitting that to himself, but he wasn't letting Tomcat know that. Then again, his body had already betrayed him big-time.

Clint. Not Tomcat. It was like he'd lost one man while another came back to claim him. So who'd been fucking him that weekend? And why did it matter so much?

Now, his body moved against Clint's mouth shamelessly. Uncontrollably. He gripped Clint's hair, unable to break the stare Clint locked him into as he came hard and his knees sagged under the fierce orgasm.

Clint pulled him in, nuzzled his cheek while he tried to get his body under control again. But the close proximity to the big man simply got him hard again.

Clint noticed immediately. "You're not scared anymore."

"You got me over that pretty fast." His eyes met Clint's, a demand for answers, an acknowledgement. Something.

The sex was supposed to be the apology—Jace got that, allowed it at first. Now he wanted more.

Clint brushed a hand over Jace's hair, which was always shaggy and falling in his eyes these days. "Is this long for a mission?"

"Yeah."

"I like it."

"I didn't do it for you." Jace pulled away, and Clint yanked him back roughly.

"I know you're pissed."

"And you're going to make it up to me with sex?" Jace asked.

"Can't think of a better way," Clint said mildly. He buried his fingers in the thick strands, tugging Jace's face closer, and this time Jace moved in faster and took control of the kiss. His tongue teased Clint's, and he grabbed the back of the man's neck to deepen the kisses.

When Jace pulled away, he was pleased to see that Clint was finally showing signs of losing control. "What do you want from me, Clint? Do you want me to tell you that it's all good—that you're forgiven? Because you still haven't told me why you're here."

Jace's eyes bored into him. The boy was going to make him say the words, and Clint couldn't blame him. Hell, even if Jace wasn't going to make him say them, Clint owed him.

Seeing the pictures of Jace visiting his fake grave in the

rain nearly killed him. Stopping the texts had been one thing, but he'd figured he'd be the only one hurting. Figured Jace could—and would—easily move on.

He hadn't told Jace about the plan, so although Jace had suspected what had really happened, Clint knew he was still freaked as hell. And pissed, although he'd tried really hard not to show it. And Clint went along with that, because if the kid wanted to pretend not to have feelings, who was he to argue?

He'd lived under that MO for years. But the tears running down Jace's cheeks were clearly visible in the pictures, and that was enough to break Clint's heart. "Like I said, I couldn't tell you anything."

"Right."

"Come on, Jace—I couldn't drag you into this. You knew too much already. You live in this world. You of all people could cut me some slack."

"I probably would've. Should. But I can't." Jace pushed away, told him, "You've got to go—I have an early morning."

"I think you can handle PT after a late night."

Jace didn't answer, just bent down to pull his sweats up. Clint yanked them out of his hand and back down again, pressed their groins together and pinned him to the counter before Jace could stop him. Clint kissed the protest out of him, and maybe, for the first time in his life, planned on apologizing to someone he might be in a relationship with.

Before this, he'd barely acknowledged the men he was with, would tell them straight out that it was all about his work and no commitments. And if they couldn't handle it—which none of them could for long, thanks to the constant missions away and barebones contact, if any at all—he moved on.

None of them could handle it except this boy, and he pulled his mouth off Jace's and whispered, "Sorry, baby," over and

SE Jakes

over into his neck. Said it until he felt Jace's body relent for the second time and then added, "I didn't think you'd find out before you got back."

"You didn't think I would've heard, no matter where I was?" Jace asked. "Or did you think I wouldn't care?"

Clint didn't want to answer that, mainly because he didn't know how to. And Jace wisely didn't push.

Clint kissed him again, his hands around the boy's hips, pulling him forward so he could finger Jace's ass, his own cock aching with need. He had lube in his pocket, because he'd known this would happen when he saw the boy, and now he snapped it open and put some on his fingers so he could enter the boy without hurting him.

Still, Jace clutched his neck, wound his calf around Clint's thigh to spread himself wider and whimpered.

"So tight. Still so goddamned tight," Clint murmured. "This is going to feel amazing around my dick, Jace. You're going to ride this cock with your tight ass over and over, and you're going to love it."

"Yeah," Jace grunted as a third finger worked inside of him, twisting, opening him...brushing his prostate and making him jump.

"You like that, pretty baby?" Clint murmured, and Jace whispered back, "Fuck you."

"Maybe later."

"Clint..." Jace said his name in a frustrated moan.

"I could do anything I wanted to you right now, couldn't I?" Clint asked. He was pushing it, but he had to. "I could hold you down and put another finger in you—maybe my whole hand, and you'd have to take it."

Jace moaned and buried his head in Clint's shoulder.

"You'd let me, wouldn't you? Even though you're pissed at me, you'd let me tie you down and you'd fuck my arm."

A strangled "Yes," came from Jace's throat, and in that instant, Clint knew he could love the man writhing under his touch. It nearly knocked him off his feet, scared him enough that he thought about running and not coming back.

Instead, without another word, he withdrew his fingers carefully and lifted Jace, threw him unceremoniously over his shoulder, asking, "Bedroom upstairs?"

"I don't need a bed. Please. Anywhere. Floor, counter, doesn't matter."

"You just got back from three months of sleeping on the ground. It matters," Clint said as he put him on the bed.

"Wait, you knew where I was?" Jace stared at him with an expression Clint couldn't quite place.

"Yeah, the entire time. Done talking for now?"

"Yeah."

"Good."

Once in Jace's bed, the two men dragged toward one another, their bodies finally crashing hard, melding together. Jace heard Clint's clothes tear, and then the man used his own ripped shirt to tie Jace's arms above his head and to the headboard.

Clint kissed him, held him, and Jace melted into his arms the way he always knew he would. He didn't know what Clint being here actually meant, didn't think he could right now. But Jace wouldn't waste a single damned minute of this time, because every fucking fantasy of his over the past months had been about this guy.

But the things he did, with his hands and tongue...Jace

was pretty sure he'd never had orgasms this damned strong, or this many. And Clint was leading him toward more, with Jace's cock in his mouth, with several of Clint's fingers in his ass, sliding back and forth, forcing Jace to work with Clint's rhythm instead of his own.

"Dammit," Jace muttered when Clint's knuckle hit his prostate, and then Clint's free hand circled the bottom of Jace's cock, stopping him from shooting. "Fucking sadist."

Clint chuckled before taking one of Jace's balls and mouthing it with just enough pressure to make him whimper. Jace tugged at his bound wrists furiously, and before he could rip the fabric, Clint was up and burying his cock inside Jace. Slow and steady but not giving him any quarter, his heavy body holding Jace's down, one hand on Jace's bound wrists to stop him from getting himself free.

"I'll tie your legs, too, if I have to," Clint told him, and the moan slipped from Jace's throat before he could stop himself.

"Fuck me now," Jace rasped.

"Demanding sort, aren't we?"

Before Jace could answer, Clint was taking him with a fervor Jace would have to fight to keep up with.

And he did.

"Now." Jace bucked up, forcing Clint's thick cock deeper. Finally, Clint rocked harder and harder into him, until Jace's balls drew up tight.

"That's it, baby. Just come," Clint urged.

"Don't you dare stop," Jace practically begged, making an effort to get the words out as Clint drove into him faster. Within minutes, Jace shot all over his stomach and chest with a loud groan.

"Don't worry, I won't stop. Got a lot of making up to do,"

Clint muttered, more to himself than to Jace, but Jace didn't plan on stopping him.

"Am I forgiven?" Clint whispered, his hand moving between their bodies to work Jace's cock.

"So not fair," Jace mumbled, or tried to, because honestly, what came out was pretty incoherent.

It made Clint smile, and the light was back in his eyes, the one that Jace swore he saw for the first time when they'd kissed in his undercover loft.

"That's not an answer," Clint persisted. "Don't make me play dirty."

Jace simply said, "Do what you have to."

Chapter Nine

Clint took that as an invitation, studied the boy as he took him again, unable to get his fill, noted every nuance, every single breath the boy took. Every reaction put on file in his memory—because he wanted to please this kid more than he'd ever pleased anyone in his life. Wanted to take him higher, make him shout Clint's name over and over, loudly enough to wake up everyone in the general vicinity. Wanted to mark him so no one else in Jace's life even came close to this fucking. Ever.

Clint was being selfish as hell, and he didn't care. He realized that he never wanted Jace to find someone else, and the possessiveness that gripped him scared the ever-living fuck out of him and made him want to hang on tighter.

This was supposed to be a one-night thing—a one-weekend thing. Officially, he was dead. But apparently Jace had the power to bring him back to life, and Clint wasn't afraid to admit that it was an excellent thing.

But for how long? This boy could easily be his kryptonite, and beyond that, time would never be on his side while he was still in the CIA. Clint was hitting his prime in the organization. There may be younger guys, but he had gotten few injuries and his field experience was priceless.

He hadn't worked this hard to throw it away, and he

already knew his bloodlines would keep him from connecting to any one person for very long.

Rex glanced at his ringing phone and saw that it was Damon. The last time he'd spoken with his friend was during the mission, weeks ago. Now, he took the call on the back deck of his house that overlooked the beach, a beer in hand, and felt the familiar anger at what Jace had been going through. The kid had done his job—an excellent job—throwing himself into the work instead of focusing on his personal life.

"I didn't say anything to him," Rex told his friend after Damon said hello.

"Clint appreciates that."

"So he finally went back to his old name? Tell him I didn't do it for him. Asshole. Hope I get the chance to tell him to his face."

Damon sighed. "What's this really about, Rex?"

"Ah, don't play amateur psychologist with me."

"I'm your friend—I don't have to play at anything. And you're wound tighter than hell, tighter than last time I saw you when you were staring at the young SEAL on your team like you wanted to lock him up and protect him from the world." Damon paused. "Hell, I want to do the same thing with Tanner, but I can't."

Rex took a long drink of beer and stared out across the dark sky, the rolling waves a soothing echo in the background. He'd known Damon for fifteen years, and even though they didn't talk often, he knew the man understood. "I want Sawyer, but—"

"You're being a complete asshole instead," Damon finished.

"I didn't think this would be that hard," Rex admitted. "I'm scared, and he's terrified. We're a couple of fucking women."

"Does he know about Josh?"

"He knows about the capture—nothing more."

"Maybe it's time he does," Damon said. "I get you're not into Domming anymore. I get that more than anyone, but those Dom instincts never really go away. They're a part of you for a reason. Call on them and see if that helps at all."

Damon had a damned good point. Rex had gone so far in the opposite direction from Domming these days, he often felt lost. Not using them with Josh, his former lover, hadn't been a problem, but in this situation, well, being in control—taking control—was probably what would be best for both him and Sawyer.

He knew Sawyer and Jace had gotten close on their first mission that had gone goatfuck. It happened right after Rex had gotten there to take charge of the team, but he hadn't been in on the planning of the mission they'd been in trouble on. They'd been lent to another team because of Sawyer's sniping abilities and Jace's expertise at demolition.

The helpless feeling of knowing those two were beyond rescue for an entire stretch of night in dangerous country had made Rex flash back to a horrible time of his own. He'd only known the two SEALs for a month, and he and Sawyer had connected instantly, an attraction he knew blew Sawyer away. He'd seen it in the boy's eyes when they'd met, when Sawyer came into his office thinking the old CO was still there—he'd been pissed and was ripping into the guy, which Rex had to admit was more than fucking fair—and when Rex had taken off his hat and turned, Sawyer's mouth kind of gaped open for a second. And it had nothing to do with being stunned that he was yelling at his new boss.

No, the attraction was palpable. Electric. Rex was still surprised they hadn't kissed at that moment. He'd never believed in anything at first sight, because even lust needed a little time to grow, but since meeting Sawyer, he'd become a convert.

And then he'd spent the rest of their time working together yelling at the kid, who wasn't really a kid at all, and wondering how Sawyer could be straight and still look at Rex the way he did.

Sawyer, with light brown hair that got streaks of blond whenever he was in the sun and a face that held enough of an edge to keep him from being classic all-American good-looking, all of which drew Rex to him constantly. Sawyer was constant movement to Rex's solid stance; they balanced each other in the field, and Rex wondered if that balance would hold up in their personal lives.

But he hadn't allowed himself to spend any off-duty time with Sawyer, held him at arm's length.

Damon broke his reverie, saying, "Just so you know, I did tell Clint what you said."

"And?"

"He's with Jace now. For better or for worse. He knows as well as the rest of us that not all secrets are meant to be kept."

At least something was right for someone on his team.

"Thanks, Damon. I'll keep that in mind," Rex told his friend before hanging up the phone...and he really tried to believe he meant it.

After they'd fucked each other senseless, Jace lay on his back on the mattress, Clint's thigh thrown across his body in a show of possession that Jace both liked and hated.

"You need more of an apology, don't you?" Clint asked.

"Don't do that shit—don't pretend you can read my mind."

Clint propped himself up on his elbow and stared down at him. "I'm not right?"

"I really thought...fuck." Jace rolled away and stared out the windows that overlooked the ocean from the second floor. He wondered why Clint's faked death had affected him so badly after only several rolls with the guy.

But hell, he'd always known it was far more than that, even before it happened. Didn't know why, and that's probably what bothered him the most.

"You can't choose who you fall in love with," Sawyer would always say, mainly to justify the fact that he was a straight guy who'd fallen in love with another man.

And now he was thinking about love and Clint in the same breath, and fuck no, it was too soon.

"If you knew, then why did you get so upset?"

Jace paused, then said, "I knew Tomcat was gone, no matter what. And I didn't know what that meant. Why it hurt so much. I didn't know if I was a part of the pretend."

"You weren't—you're not. For me, it wasn't an ending—it was a beginning, although you know my job and the limits it puts on me."

"What, exactly, does that mean?"

"For one thing, discretion."

"So if the CIA comes calling..."

"They won't. They shouldn't. But I could get fucked for this involvement with you if something goes wrong."

Jace got it—he was still in the MC. And involved with the

Feds, and fuck, this could go bad if he let it. Which he wouldn't. "So what, every time you're in town, we get together?"

"It's a start. I don't think either of us is able to do anything more at the moment."

Jace nodded, because he wasn't.

Clint touched his shoulder. "Jace—"

"Don't, okay? I'm angrier at myself."

"Why?"

He stopped himself from saying *Because I fell for you like a girl.* "I just am, all right?"

There was a long pause, and then Clint admitted, "I'm pissed that I'm here, too, Jace."

"What's with you and the mind reading?"

"You don't have a poker face. At least not with me. Look, not contacting you was really hard—I didn't expect it to be. It shouldn't have been. I never should've texted you, but I couldn't help it. I played all of this badly."

"So what do we do?"

Clint ran a hand through his hair. "Mind if I stay here with you until I get called?"

It could be hours or days. Jace hoped for the latter. "Yeah. Just don't expect me to cook for you or anything."

Clint rolled his eyes. "Wouldn't dream of it," he said as he moved to get up, searched for his pants.

"And once this time is up, then what?"

Clint turned from where he'd been rooting around on the floor, because he'd actually planned to do some cooking for Jace. "What do you want to happen?"

"You're the one who came back to find me," Jace pointed

out. "You could've stayed dead and buried. I can't believe you couldn't find another lay without complications."

Clint wanted to give a quick answer, about how Jace was in fact a hell of a lay, but a wiseass comment refused to fly from his usually quick-witted mouth.

Because Jace asked the question he'd refused to ask himself. Why *had* he come here? Jace would've gotten over him, gotten on with his work and his life—Clint was for sure nothing but a huge complication in Jace's life.

Or is it the other way around?

Because Jace was probably the best kind of complication to have. "My job," he started.

Jace cut him off. "Mine, too."

"I can't tell if that makes it better or worse," Clint admitted.

"Maybe you should stay in bed until we figure it out."

Clint dropped his clothes back to the floor and moved next to Jace again. "That's not a half-bad idea."

Chapter Ten

Sawyer slammed into the locker room and away from Rex's yelling. He'd stayed behind to work on some maneuvers after most of the team went home, and now he wished he'd followed them. But the perfectionist in him wanted better—and Jace stayed with him—and so they'd worked until he was sweating and dizzy, until his arms felt like rubber, and still it wasn't enough.

To top it off, Rex wasn't finished chewing his ass out.

"Don't you walk away from me," he drawled, and dammit, the man didn't have to yell to yell, his deep voice doing more damage to Sawyer than any kind of scream could.

Sawyer steeled himself and turned to see the big man with the shaved head and the dark eyes staring him down. "You already pointed out how I fucked up, *sir*. I told you it wouldn't happen again." And it hadn't, the next twelve times Rex had made Sawyer repeat the maneuver. But that wasn't going to satisfy the man at all.

Even Jace coming in behind Rex didn't stop the berating, and finally, Rex left and Sawyer went into the shower and wondered if he'd ever please the one man he so desperately wanted to please.

"You all right?" Jace asked from the next shower stall.

"Great."

"It wasn't all your fuck-up—he was pissed that the team left."

That was the truth—the entire team had screwed up and should've had the sense to stay and show their CO they were up to the extra challenge, but somehow, when that failed to happen, it was Sawyer's fault. And the thing was, no one was more pissed about the fuck-up than Sawyer himself. He wanted to be the best, trained long and hard for it, and was probably harder on himself than Rex ever would be.

Hearing about Clint coming back from the dead was the only bright spot in the day—and it was nice to see his friend happy, albeit reserved. Jace told Sawyer he was planning on holding back because he didn't want to go through more shit with Clint.

"You want to hang out tonight?" Jace asked.

"No, I want you to hang out with Clint," Sawyer told him as he toweled off and dressed. Jace had told him about Clint's return that morning, and hell, he'd never seen the guy so happy, but still slightly guarded. But from everything Jace mentioned, it sounded like things between the men were good.

Unlike things between him and Rex. "I'll be all right."

Jace paused. "Look, I think—"

"Forget it."

"I don't get what the problem is. I mean, you're worried—I get that—but—"

"At first, I was scared—confused—yeah. But then I got some more information and it threw me."

Jace waited patiently and Sawyer looked around before he said, "You know about Rex's capture, right?"

"Everyone knows."

"I heard from someone who knew him and his team back in

the day. And I think that maybe he was involved with one of the guys who was killed on that mission."

"Fuck," Jace breathed.

"Yeah." Sawyer shook his head. Competing with a ghost wasn't something he was prepared to do. He'd had a ringside seat to that with his mother when she'd remarried. His stepfather was great, but there was nothing he could do that would ever make her forget her first love.

Sawyer knew, because she told him so every opportunity she had toward the end of their relationship, when Sawyer was sixteen and the fighting had gotten so bad he'd moved out to his grandparents' house. "How do I know he's over that? My grandmother used to say that you never forget your first love—that most people never get over it."

Jace, who knew what Sawyer had grown up with, told him, "You don't know if that's his first love—or if that's how he feels."

No, that was true, but it wasn't a pattern he wanted to repeat. "Thanks for listening. Go home and have fun, all right? I'll work something out."

Jace did so reluctantly and only when Sawyer urged him harder. Sawyer didn't want anyone to have to sit around and deal with his moods, which was pretty damned ironic considering those roles were usually reversed.

He went home and stewed for a bit before deciding he needed to get out before the walls closed in on him. He got up the nerve to go where he'd been thinking about going for the past several months, although maybe it wasn't nerve so much as plain, old-fashioned anger.

The club was close to base but on the other end of town from where he usually hung out, and supposedly very gay-military friendly. Maybe a little too much for Sawyer at this point—he hadn't been expecting to be looked up and down as much as he was. He went to a corner of the bar where the sympathetic bartender poured him a beer and said, "It's always hard when you're new."

Sawyer nodded and played with the bottle. He did a low-key survey of the room and wondered if there was anyone here who'd be surprised to see him.

Maybe he needed to get the edge off before he approached Rex. Going to the man as a total novice to all this wasn't very appealing, he figured, and if he could get some experience, maybe he'd have the balls to talk to Rex about how he felt.

"How's it going?" The man who slid into the seat next to him was a pilot from the Virginia base. "I'm Carter."

"Sawyer."

"I've seen you around. SEAL, right?"

"Yeah."

"First time here?"

Sawyer nodded.

"Well, glad you came." Carter's lips twisted suggestively, and Sawyer wished he were attracted to the guy. But no, there was nothing.

Just then, an electric pull turned his head toward the back door of the bar, and his stomach tightened when he saw Rex there. If his CO noticed him, he didn't act like it. No, he continued whatever he was doing, his hand casually on the back of a younger man's neck as he talked to a small group of men.

He turned around and ran his own hand over the back of his neck, wishing he was the one standing in that guy's place. Wondered how Rex's hand would feel on him when it wasn't during PT and involving yelling.

This had been a big goddamned mistake. Although, if he

was honest with himself, he would've hoped to run into Rex, but that was a pipe dream. And in that dream, things would've gone well. Rex would've approached him and the walls would've fallen down and everything would've been so easy.

But nothing about this was.

He motioned for the bartender, suddenly intent on getting hammered and going home with Carter, as though the combination might make everything better, even though he knew it wouldn't.

Rex knew Sawyer was there—spotted the back of the light brown head with the blond sun streaks the second Sawyer had walked in and nearly went over and dragged the boy out. But then he decided to see just what in the hell Sawyer was trying to pull.

Now Rex cornered him in the back hallway near the bathroom, which gave them a slight bit of privacy. Still, he kept his voice down and demanded, "What the hell are you doing here, Sawyer?"

"I didn't realize I wasn't allowed to come here," Sawyer shot back. "I've got someone waiting for me."

"Yeah, I saw Carter." Rex wouldn't let anything happen between the boy and the pilot if he had to hogtie Sawyer and take him out of here.

And lose your goddamned job.

"Don't you go home with him."

"Is that a direct order?"

Rex's eyes narrowed. "Yes, it is."

"What do you care?" Sawyer demanded. "Because if we're talking don't ask, don't tell—"

"I thought you were straight," Rex said, because he wanted

to hear it from Sawyer that he wasn't.

"I thought so, too," Sawyer said, and looked like he wanted to take it back immediately. But it had been the truth that poured out of his mouth.

It was only then that Rex finally realized that Sawyer wasn't trying to pull a fast one. For as brave a man as he was, he was terrified, and Rex nearly reached out to comfort him but stopped. Because Sawyer would hate the coddling more than anything. No, he needed to be pushed past his comfort level until he was so pissed that he'd make the first move.

And Rex knew just how to play that. "How are things with Jace?"

Sawyer eyed him with slight suspicion. "He's all right."

"Why isn't he here with you?"

"He's busy."

"This isn't you. You're straight, so why are you coming here, letting men pick you up?"

"You think you've got all the answers," the boy challenged him.

Rex stared at him for a long moment before asking, "What are the answers you want me to have, Sawyer?"

What are the answers you want me to have, Sawyer?

Rex's voice was a slow, honeyed drawl. Sawyer had heard it a thousand times in his dreams, giving both commands and comfort. And now, he was a stone's throw away, and Sawyer had consumed enough liquid courage to tell him exactly what he wanted.

But one look into Rex's deep, dark eyes and all Sawyer could see was his career going up in smoke. Because if he misjudged this one, he'd never live it down professionally.

"Gotta go," he muttered and pushed past Rex.

Sawyer had to get the hell out of there. Watching his CO stroll out of the bathroom and then talk easily with everyone *but* him was killing Sawyer—and he'd been in a shitty enough mood already.

Beyond that, by the time he got back to Carter, it was obvious that the SEAL CO had threatened the shit out of the pilot, because Carter was cordial but the friendliness had dried up.

He was already by the back door, and so he slid outside after telling Carter thanks for hanging out with him. It was freezing cold, mid-January, and the frigid air was sobering him up fast. The walk of a couple of miles would do him good, so he stuck his hands in his pockets, cut across and headed down the second alleyway toward the main street.

He stopped when he heard the footsteps. He wasn't in the mood to fend off muggers or assholes who decided it was fun to pick a fight with a military guy.

Finally, when the footsteps were close enough, he turned fast, found himself pinned to the side of the brick building by Rex.

Fuck. He struggled to get away before he got hard, but it was too late. The man's body pressed his, thigh to thigh, chest to chest. Groin to groin, and a picture flashed in his mind of them against this wall with no clothing between them, with Rex's mouth on his, hand on his cock...

"What the fuck are you doing?" he asked, with the thin hope Rex wouldn't notice his arousal. But the way Rex pressed him, Sawyer knew he did. Maybe he knew and thought Sawyer's stupid crush was something to humiliate him with.

It sure as shit worked. Rex, in the meantime, continued to study his face, and who knew what he was searching for?

"Rex, get the hell off me." Because fuck protocol.

Rex shifted, then pressed harder, and finally, Sawyer noticed something he hadn't at first.

Rex was turned on, too. This wasn't about humiliation, or maybe it was, because then Rex said, "I know you watched me in the shower that night—you thought I didn't know you were there."

It had happened months earlier. Rex, in the small, portable shower in the middle of the desert training camp at midnight. Sawyer had gone in there because he'd been too hot to sleep— and then he'd gotten even hotter when he'd watched Rex stroking his cock.

The man had thrown his head back when he'd climaxed, bared his teeth as come shot from him in thick, white spurts, and Sawyer had thought about what it would've felt like to be on his knees in front of him, swallowing it. Having Rex come in his ass. That had been the night he'd known for sure he wanted the man. Before that, it was speculation, an aberration, since he'd never been attracted to men before.

After that shower, he'd wanted no one but Rex.

"Did you like it?" Rex continued. "You stayed until I came. Did you go back to your tent and touch yourself, thinking about me?"

He had. Quietly, under the covers, since he wasn't alone in the bunk. He'd stroked his cock and imagined Rex on top of him, telling him he was going to fuck him, that he didn't care if anyone else was watching, that Sawyer needed to be quiet or everyone would know...

"You're thinking about it, aren't you?" Rex laughed softly, his eyes dark with desire, and the heat rose up around them until Sawyer was pretty sure there was steam coming off them.

He swallowed hard, unable to breathe or form any kind of

coherent thought. Rex's scent swirled around him—a mixture of musk and man and winter. Rex always reminded him of the best parts of winter air—he'd bet the man tasted crisp and cool with a bite that tingled almost painfully on your skin.

Finally, his CO said, "What do *you* want, Sawyer?"

What a question. Sawyer swallowed hard and wished he wasn't such a coward.

"To go home," he managed.

Rex opened his mouth and closed it. Released Sawyer. As Sawyer started to walk away, Rex called, "I'm your superior. It wouldn't be wise of me to make the first move."

When Sawyer turned back, Rex was gone.

Chapter Eleven

Jace found Sawyer half-frozen on his stoop. From Sawyer's expression, it was obvious he knew what he'd interrupted, but Jace insisted, "What the hell, man? Get in here," even as Sawyer started backing up.

Jace hiked up his sweats and grabbed for the guy, but Sawyer said, "Shit, I'll just call a cab—"

"Get the fuck in here, all right?" Jace was finally able to tug him in from the cold. "What were you thinking, walking home in this?"

"I was trying not to think."

Clint had already moved to find his own clothes in the living room, had left the two of them alone as Jace attempted to shake off his sex haze and help his friend.

"So I guess you've pretty much forgiven him," Sawyer said wryly. "So much for holding back."

Jace snorted. "Come sit down—you need coffee."

"I'm not that drunk. Maybe a little. Or maybe I should drink more." Sawyer slid into a kitchen chair and put his head down on the table.

It was obvious his friend had walked pretty damned far—his lips were practically blue, and he didn't say anything for a long while after Jace pushed coffee into him, just lifted his head and stared into space.

Finally, Jace came out and asked, "Did you see Rex tonight?"

Sawyer's gaze cut to him, and Jace was relieved to see that some of the fog had lifted. "Yeah. I went to Deels."

The bar was gay friendly, and to Jace's knowledge, Sawyer had never gone before. "You should've let me go with you."

"You were, ah, busy." Sawyer shrugged and looked around like Clint was in the room.

It didn't take much to get him to spill what happened at the bar.

"I still can't believe you went there, man. What did you think would happen?"

Sawyer shrugged. "I figured maybe I'd be attracted to someone else. And I left being more attracted to him. Fuck."

"And you just let him walk away?" Jace persisted, and Sawyer nodded miserably.

"I totally fucked up, right?"

"You're not a mind reader," Jace said fiercely, and yeah, things weren't completely smoothed over between him and Clint if the anger could rise in him that quickly.

Sawyer knew it too, asked, "Are we talking about me or Clint?"

Jace shrugged and stared into his coffee like it held all the answers as Sawyer continued, "I thought things were okay between you guys."

Jace had thought so as well, until he'd realized there was so little he knew about Clint. "Things are fine, I guess. Just...you know...confusing sometimes."

"How about asking?" Sawyer suggested.

Jace leaned back and laughed. "We're such fucking guys."

"What gave it away?" Sawyer asked. "He's going to think I'm a fucking idiot."

"He's going to know you're scared."

Clint's voice had come from the doorway, and Sawyer froze before saying, "This just isn't my night."

Jace glanced back at Clint. "He's right."

"Great." Sawyer stood and held out his hand. "Sawyer."

Clint took it, introduced himself and then grabbed Jace's coffee and finished it before pouring more. "Didn't mean to intrude."

"'S'all right. Shouldn't be mooning about this shit anyway." Sawyer ran a hand through his hair. "I'll call a cab."

"You can crash here," Jace offered.

"Don't leave on my account," Clint said. "Want pizza if I order?"

"I could eat," Sawyer said, and Jace nodded.

"Of course you could. Between you and Jace, I'll need five pies if I want a slice," he muttered, but there was a small smile on his face, and Jace shrugged because that was probably true.

While they ate, Clint regaled them with stories from his Delta days, even managing to slip in some stuff about Rex that made Sawyer grin instead of look unhappy. Afterward, Sawyer slept on the pull-out downstairs and Jace followed Clint into the bedroom.

"Thanks for being so good to my friend."

"I like him. I like knowing you have good people watching your six."

"We almost died on one of our recent missions—the one right before I slept with you the first time," Jace blurted out. He told Clint the story and ended with, "That's why I kept my end of the bargain after hesitating for so long."

Clint looked shaken. He obviously knew the kind of danger Jace dealt with on a regular basis, but knowing it and hearing an actual truth were two different things. "That's why the thing with Rex is weighing on him so much."

"Part of it."

"And the other part is the CO thing?"

"Yeah. But the biggest problem is that he's straight."

Clint's eyebrows rose. "Bullshit."

"Nah, it's true. I think he just fell in love. Didn't know how to handle it. I told him to just go for it, and look how it ended up."

Clint pulled Jace to him. "It doesn't sound like it's an ending at all. I'd say it was a beginning."

Jace wasn't sure if he was talking about Sawyer and Rex or them, and decided that, either way, it didn't matter.

Rex still smelled Sawyer on him; the younger man always smelled so damned good, and he didn't know why everyone else hadn't noticed it.

Actually, he was damned grateful—because if anyone else had shown the least bit of interest in Sawyer over the past months when he'd woken up nightly, frustrated and alone, he probably would've punched them out. He barely fought that urge with Carter, who'd gotten the message pretty quick.

And you're still alone, he reminded himself. Dammit. He could feel Sawyer's cock rubbing his—the boy was so concerned about revealing his feelings and being rejected—or worse—that he hadn't noticed Rex had been rock hard, too. And when he'd finally told Sawyer the deal, he couldn't stick around and wait, because he didn't want to come on too strong.

Rex had been assigned to this particular SEAL team because of his old CO, who thought he'd be a perfect fit for the relatively young team—Rex had a lot to offer in terms of experience, and that was an invaluable part of training. The mission Sawyer and Jace had become friends on happened a month after Rex took command, which was nearly four years after his capture and triumphant return to the SEAL teams.

From the second he'd met Sawyer, there was something about the SEAL that had intrigued him. Yeah, he knew Sawyer was straight—but Sawyer had looked at him like he'd seen a ghost before he'd recovered.

But now he was sure the boy had feelings for him beyond sexual ones, hadn't been surer of anything in his entire life. And as he lay here, the clock reading two a.m. and sleep obviously not his friend, he tried not to think about the one hundred and thirty-nine days he'd done this when he'd been imprisoned, without the aid of a clock or a mattress or any other comforts he enjoyed.

The prison in a South American jungle had consisted of many small cells—he couldn't stand up in the one he'd been placed in. There were four SEALs captured that mission, and the enemy soldiers had spread the wealth of the torture over all of them equally. But Josh, his teammate, had an infection that would never have healed under the primitive conditions, and as much as Rex begged for a doctor for him—and he did beg, no matter that it set his teeth on edge—no medical help ever arrived. The soldiers burned Josh's body, so there was nothing of the man to bring home.

Rex still felt that loss acutely.

Josh had been more than a teammate for four solid years,

since the first month he and Rex had served together. Both old enough to know that chances like that weren't something to be passed up, they'd fallen into a hot, happy relationship that would've gotten both of them court-martialed if anyone found out.

No one had.

Goddamn, he could barely remember what life had been like after Josh and before Sawyer, because he'd lived those years in a personal fog, while professionally, his focus was laser-like and his career soared as a result.

Professionally he was fulfilled, but he wanted personal fulfillment, too. Wanted Sawyer to be the one to help him with that.

The other two men he'd been captured with were no longer in the Navy—one retired by choice, the other forced out because his arms never healed properly after having been broken during the torture. Having to consider himself lucky was an odd choice of words, but there was no other explanation. And so he was left with memories and broad stripes from the whip along his back and the backs of his thighs that would never heal into smooth skin.

Every lover who touched him from here on out would know, and he had never really cared. But he did with Sawyer, and he wasn't sure why. He figured Sawyer had heard rumors about what had happened to Rex, but to show him...fuck, Rex hadn't been this shy since he was seventeen, when he hit his first gay club and knew what he wanted. The Navy was a strange choice for a gay man, but he'd always been a physical guy, and the SEALs provided him with an excellent outlet.

When he was in the cell, all he thought about—beyond escape—was the fact that he'd lost Josh and that Josh was probably somewhere on the other side, willing him to survive.

If Rex closed his eyes, he could clearly see the image of the fantasy that had gotten him through a lot of lonely nights over the past year.

It happened in the sand pit—Iraq. The team had a stop there for a month after a recon mission. The team shared a tent, and he'd gotten his own, but the showers were communal, except for two set up with only cool water between his tent and his team's. His favorite thing to do was go in there around midnight and beat off under the spray—it was the only thing that put him to sleep.

He'd been midstroke when he'd suddenly known he wasn't alone any longer. He really didn't give a shit who watched him beat off—there were a lot of gay or bi guys in the military, and notwithstanding, they were all undersexed and horny as hell.

He'd lowered his head and checked out who was watching him from under his lashes—he'd have known Sawyer anywhere. It helped that he'd been wearing the old boots with the rip in the front that he kept duct-taping shut because he couldn't get new ones to fit his size fourteen feet until they got home.

He imagined that Sawyer approached him, and fuck, what he'd do to the boy...maybe drag him under the spray, press him to his knees and force his cock down Sawyer's throat. Or maybe he'd strip his pants off and take him, bent over in the shower, where anyone could walk in and find them.

He'd come so hard he saw stars...and only then did Sawyer's boots retreat.

He'd bet neither one of them got any sleep that night.

He'd also bet the same tonight. And he was too restless not to do something about it.

He'd Dommed before, never wanting the lifestyle like some of the men he was friends with. He'd met Clint on a joint mission with Delta and the SEALs and discovered they had the same bent. Clint had gotten him access to some of the more exclusive clubs, and while Rex enjoyed catting around, he'd always felt like he was missing a limb.

Now, he figured he could use a few of those techniques to get this party started and pull Sawyer closer to confessing his feelings. Because despite what he'd told Sawyer about not being able to make the first move, life was too short not to try to encourage the boy.

He reached out and dialed Sawyer's number, pretty sure the boy wouldn't be asleep.

His hello was tentative. Rex didn't hesitate in saying, "You're going to do everything I say—understand?"

"Rex—"

"It's a yes or a no."

A long pause and then a whispered, "Yes," made Rex's heart start beating again.

"Good. Now, put your hand around your cock." There was a small whimper on the other end of the line that made Rex smile and grab his own dick. "Did you do it?"

"Yes."

"That's the operative word for this call, understood?"

"Yes."

"Did you like when I pressed against you?"

"Yes."

"Did you beat off already tonight thinking about me?"

There was a long pause and then, "I wanted to, but I'm not exactly home."

Rex forced his jealousy down. It wasn't a yes answer, but he let it go because he wanted to know more. "Where are you?"

"I, ah, ended up at Jace's. I'm on his pull-out couch."

Rex relaxed again. "Ready to get rid of some of that tension?"

"Yeah."

He let the slang go. "Good. Now I want a longer answer. Stroke yourself, close your eyes and imagine seeing me in the shower in Iraq." Rex heard a long, stuttered breath from the boy and knew he could come from that sound alone. "You think about that a lot, don't you?"

"Yes."

"What exactly do you think about?"

"Rex, I—"

"Tell me." The command in his voice jump-started Sawyer's confession.

"Instead of just watching, I strip and walk over to you," he said quickly. "You're surprised to see me there—and I think you're going to yell at me, because you always yell at me, but you don't."

Rex closed his eyes and tried not to wince at the yelling part, because hell, he deserved that one. "Keep going. And be prepared to come whenever I tell you to."

"Okay." A hard swallow and then, "You grab me, pull me close. And then you...kiss me. And fuck, it's good, Rex. So damned good."

Sawyer's voice caught, and Rex let him remain silent for a little while, just the heavy breathing across the line connecting them to each other. And then, without further pushing, Sawyer started talking again.

"When you break the kiss, I push you to your knees and I grab your shoulders and pull you close to my dick," he said, and Rex's eyes opened in surprise. So the boy had a little kink of his own, did he? Maybe he wasn't as submissive as Rex thought—and that was damned appealing as well.

"Are you scared?"

"Yeah, a little. But I know you'll take care of me. And you take my cock into your mouth and I have to grab on to your shoulders so I don't fall, because it feels so good. And I come—right away—because it's you. And it's what I've wanted for so long. But you're not upset. You just take everything I give and then you...fuck..."

He'd come—without Rex telling him to, and Rex stroked himself with a few hard tugs and joined him, the groans similar to the ones he'd had in Iraq that night. And even though the silence was between them, it was comfortable as the men caught their breaths and Rex reveled in the post-orgasm haze.

"We'll do this again, Sawyer, after you get back from Coronado training," Rex promised. "Remember where you left off."

"Rex, I'm not sure—" Sawyer started to tell him.

"I know. But this is a start." He hung up before either of them said anything more to ruin what had just happened, and, for the first time in years, he fell into a contented sleep.

They had a week together before Clint had to leave for his next assignment. A week of Clint lazing around Jace's house while the boy went to base daily for PT and other training, came home to a good meal and a good fuck.

Man, he could get used to this.

Jace had gotten home from base a couple of hours earlier, was now quietly watching Clint pack up.

"I'm sure you're headed out soon, too," Clint said finally, and handed Jace a phone number.

SE Jakes

"What's this?"

"A service. For both of us. Call in, leave a message and I'll get back to you no matter where I am or what phone I'm using. Same to you."

Jace nodded. "I like that."

"Good." He ran a thumb across the boy's bottom lip. "I can't promise you more than this, because—"

"This is good enough for right now," Jace assured him.

"Good."

At this point, they both knew it was all they could have. Their jobs took them to dangerous places they couldn't tell anyone about, and neither man was ready to give that up and settle down. At least that's what Clint told himself Jace was thinking, because he was perilously close to thinking that maybe, just maybe, he could have some kind of life outside of the CIA—and he'd always known that just wasn't possible.

Chapter Twelve

Jace called Kenny to meet him for a quick bite to eat in order to fill the hours until night training, when he realized he'd been aching since Clint left.

He'd been doing his job, dealing with Kenny, pretending everything was business as usual while inside he felt like something was missing.

And someone was. Clint had only been gone a week, but it felt like far longer, despite the texts and the call he'd managed.

It had been so much easier when Jace believed it would be all about getting his sexual appetites slaked, when fucking and being held by Clint was all Jace thought he needed. When he hadn't imagined anything beyond the physical, of course, since that need had been the greatest. Or at least he'd thought it had been. He was all kinds of turned around now.

And even then, Jace had been fooling himself, because he knew he'd want more. But in order to get more, he'd have to share bits of himself. And he'd been guarded as anything for as long as he could remember.

Changing wasn't going to happen soon—or easily. He couldn't get pissed at Clint for not sharing much when he was holding back everything, too, and not just the Fed stuff, which wasn't technically his fault. No, his background, his needs beyond the sexual—all of that was held tightly inside, partly because every time they saw each other, it took a little while to right their footing. Sex helped and was always the most immediate need, but it was like getting to know Clint all over again, and vice versa. Their missions changed them, sometimes in imperceptible ways, and there was no SOP for this relationship. No rulebook.

"Hey, cuz—you look good. Happy, for a change," Kenny noted, and Jace realized that yeah, it had been a long time since he'd been happy.

"Work's been good," was how he answered, avoiding anything personal, because even though they were family, they'd never done personal. Sure, Kenny could talk for hours about the women he banged—his term, not Jace's—because he wore the leather vest, and Jace bit his tongue instead of telling him to get checked out at the free clinic.

He listened to Kenny talk about women and the club in general, hoping to glean anything he could. Kenny told Jace a couple of months ago that Cools had taken him aside and warned him not to say anything to Jace about any of the discussions held about the club's activities.

For your cousin's safety, Cools had emphasized, and Kenny was now worried about everything he said to Jace about the MC. Granted, he still let shit slip, especially about his new job with them, and Jace carefully committed the dates to memory. The new job involved gun-running out of the new warehouse set up after the CIA had raided the first one. Jace had a strong suspicion the CIA had set this up purposely to lure the Killers and the Colombians right into their waiting hands, but he refused to say anything to the Feds about that, because it felt like a betrayal of Clint. He'd have to find another way.

He just hoped to hell that if he was right, Clint would give him fair warning to get Kenny out of the way somehow. Clint had intimated that he was keeping tabs on the job, still guiding the DEA within the structures he'd learned of during his time on the inside of the MC.

He wondered if there was going to come a point in time where he would just have to let Kenny make his own mistakes and pay the price of them without Jace's aid.

"Just the dates, Kenny—so I can make sure I'm around if you get into trouble with the law," Jace told him, and Kenny couldn't argue with that.

After half an hour, a couple of the Killers rode up in full gear.

"I told them I'd be here with you," Kenny said, and Jace cursed inwardly.

Half the people who were sitting at tables in the outside portion of the burger joint got up and left, mainly those with kids, while many of the girls and women stayed, lowered their shirts a little so their breasts jutted, licked their lips and seemed to cry out for the attention.

Jace wanted to tell them that none of them should want the kind of attention this lifestyle would bring them, but he had enough trouble with the one idiot he was sitting next to.

Kenny waved to them, and Jace tensed like there was an imminent firefight in his future.

Nacho and Shaz tapped fists with both men, sat next to Kenny and ate off his plate but didn't dare touch Jace's.

"Your cousin's been making a name for himself," Nacho told him. High-school dropout with no life outside the gang, he was taking Kenny a little too much under his wing.

Jace should've brought Kenny into the military with him. Should've insisted on it. He just kept eating while they talked sports and fucking and riding until a subject that made his blood run cold came up.

"Wait, back up on that," he said, and Nacho looked at him warily.

"Cage fighting—Kenny's up next week. We're training him for the big night."

It took everything Jace had not to smash Nacho's forehead into the table. Kenny avoided looking at Jace, because he knew his cousin was seething.

Kenny knew some basic bar-fighting moves, but cage fighting was serious business around here. Totally illegal, off-the-charts violent, with an anything-goes attitude, and Kenny didn't need to lose any more brain cells.

"You'd be a shoo-in," Nacho told Jace now. "Too bad. Although you could do it and just not tell anyone who you are."

There was no use explaining that his hands were registered deadly weapons for a reason, that he could kill a man so many different ways that he couldn't even pretend it would be a fair fight. Rules were in place for a reason—men in his job had fought before—innocent bar fights—and they'd killed men accidentally, because judging their own strength against an untrained opponent just wasn't something they could always control.

"Yeah, think of all the money we could pull down," Shaz was adding. "Jace, what if you just teach us some of your moves?"

"I'm sure Cools has some." Jace shoved his food away. He'd lost his appetite. "Gotta head out. Talk soon."

He didn't look back at the table of assholes, was heading to evening training hours earlier than necessary just to get his head back on straight after this little meeting of the minds. Maybe Sawyer was around.

But apparently it was going to be an entire day of assholes, because his handler rang him up when he was almost to base.

Mike didn't want to hear that he hadn't been able to glean much intel. The whole thing was like walking over a live landmine. There was no way you weren't going to take a hit, no matter how carefully you stepped.

"Tell me you've got something for me, Jace," Mike said in that I-just-want-to-help-you-out bullshit tone.

He told Mike about the dates for the newest runs.

"That's it?"

"Ah, fuck, Mike, that's enough. I've been away."

"What do you know about that Tomcat guy who was murdered?" Mike asked him, and Jace's hands tightened on the wheel. "Trying to figure out if he was the real deal."

"He was."

"You're sure?"

"You don't think I can spot an undercover?"

"Because if he was, we'd have to know."

Jace flashed his ID to the guard at the side gate and drove through base to get to the SEALs training center, telling Mike evenly, "He was an enforcer. This wasn't his first turn with a gang. I talked with him a few times since he was former military, but he never gave me any details because he knew I was active duty."

Mike sighed. "Jace, we need more from you if you're ever going to get your cousin free."

Making a deal with the Feds was the worst thing Jace could've done, but desperation did funny things to a man, especially when family was involved. "I'm trying, but if I push, it's too obvious. Kenny's not trained enough to play it right. I'll get the intel, but it's not my full-time job. You knew that—and I gave you good intel about that first warehouse."

"The CIA moved on it first."

"That's not my problem—you sat on it for three months. Don't sit on those dates—you'll catch the Colombians through the guns." Jace didn't give a shit about the Colombians—and this intel he just gave Mike would keep the Feds from the new warehouse and some possible DEA and CIA undercovers.

"We want something bigger."

"Fine." He blew out a harsh breath. "They're doing cage fighting. You can arrest some of them there."

"We're not interested in that."

"Maybe there are people out there who are," Jace pushed back.

"If you try to get out of this—or get another agency involved—we'll expose your cousin," Mike told him, almost pleasantly.

"I don't like threats, Mike."

"Think of it as a promise. Because if Kenny's known as a Fed snitch, don't you think the club might look at you differently?"

Jace knew that was coming—the Feds could be brutal with their witnesses if it helped them meet their ends. Tying Jace to Clint—especially his alias of Tomcat—could get the man in trouble with the CIA, as Clint had already mentioned to him. Clint had done several things the CIA wouldn't be happy with, first and foremost revealing his undercover status.

Jace hung up the phone without saying another word.

Sawyer had gone from Jace's couch to his house, where he packed quickly and headed out to a special training assignment in Coronado for the next month. It had been planned for a while, and Sawyer threw himself into the training for the first week, learning a new and complex set of rifles they were testing for accuracy.

He'd just gotten back to his private quarters around midnight and collapsed onto the shitty cot when his phone rang.

It was Rex. He stared at the phone for a long moment, wondering if he'd actually dreamed the last call that had him jerking off while Jace and Clint fucked upstairs. At least he knew there was no way they'd heard him.

He answered with a "Hey."

"Do you remember where you were?" Rex started.

Sawyer decided that there was no reason to hold back, at least not over the phone. He'd had a long day, his muscles were like jelly and the two beers he'd had gave him that nice semi-sleepy feeling. "Fuck yeah, I remember. Can't stop thinking about it."

Rex paused, and then he gave a low laugh, like he approved. "I hope your pants are off."

Sawyer shucked them quickly, got under the covers enough so he could pull them up and over him in case someone busted down the door. There was music playing from his next-door neighbor loud enough to make him comfortable. "They're off. I've been hard since I saw it was you calling."

"Good. Tell me where we were."

He closed his eyes and he was back there instantly. "I'd just come—in your mouth. You were kneeling in front of me in the shower."

"You're still hard, Sawyer."

"You get off your knees and you kiss me. I wish I knew

what that felt like..." Sawyer trailed off for a second and reflected on the night Rex pressed him to the wall, wished he hadn't been so goddamned thrown so he could've enjoyed the feel of the man's body against his more.

"It would be good, Sawyer," Rex said quietly. "Really good. What happens next?"

"God, Rex—it's so fucking good, and I came again while we were kissing. I couldn't help it, and you knew. You're rubbing the come on my chest and stomach while you're kissing me. And then you're playing with my ass, and Jesus..."

"Don't you come yet, Sawyer."

"I won't." He grunted a little and then continued, "You turn me around so I'm facing the wall and you kick my legs apart. And I think you're going to just bend me over and fuck me...but you sink to your knees instead."

Jesus H. Christ. Was he going too far?

"Is that what you want, Sawyer? Me kneeling between your legs, eating your ass until you scream?" Rex asked, his honeyed drawl husky now, and no, not too far at all.

Sawyer's breath hitched. "Yeah. You bury your face in my ass, and I'm embarrassed but I fucking love it. I'm biting my hand so I don't yell out and wake anyone up, and your tongue is..."

"Inside your ass, moving in and out until your balls tighten," Rex said. "And you taste nice, Sawyer. I can't get enough of your ass, and I'm eating you until you're begging me to stop or go—you don't know what you want. But I know how close you're getting..."

"Rex, please." His cock was leaking, and he was barely holding on.

"You taste so goddamned good, boy. I could spend hours

worshipping you like this."

Sawyer couldn't do much but pant at this point, and he knew that if Rex could do this to him with mere words, the real thing would be incredible.

"You're worried someone will catch us, right?" Rex asked.

"Uh-huh," he managed.

"I wouldn't care. I might invite them in to do just that. It would be a damned good show, watching you helpless, embarrassed at how much you love me licking your ass..."

Sawyer forced himself not to come. Delaying gratification would make everything that much sweeter.

"What if someone else wanted a turn, Sawyer?"

He heard himself actually whimper in response, and Rex chuckled lightly.

"Come, Sawyer. Right now," Rex said, and he did, harder than he had the last time, biting down a yell that could've easily escaped since he'd lost all touch with his surroundings for the past moments. When he came back down to earth, he heard Rex's harsh breaths and knew the man had come, too.

For a while they lay there, recovering, together but still apart, and then Sawyer asked, "What you said, about letting someone else..."

"Fantasy, boy. I don't like to share, but I'm all for talking about it just to get you to make those sounds. Get some sleep, and come home soon," Rex said.

Sawyer actually swore he heard Rex smile through the phone.

Sawyer slept with the phone next to him for the rest of the night.

Chapter Thirteen

Clint was on three assignments back to back which had him in Yemen, Bosnia and then Afghanistan, and now, two weeks later, he was back in his apartment, which still wasn't much of a home. He'd come to associate that with Jace's house. Wondered if Jace would care if he broke in and stayed there.

He read back over the texts Jace sent him, the one that read, *You fucked me because I saved your life? That's the worst excuse ever for being horny,* making him smile every time.

Every time he tried to put some distance between them, he realized how weak he really was. He worried about Jace nearly nonstop, scanned the news for any hint that something was wrong in the world.

The worse something was, the more of a likelihood that Jace would be there.

Jace had been gone for a week—texts were few and far between from him, but Clint did as promised and texted a check-in daily. Checked the phone for messages several times a day, just in case, although he knew the boy wouldn't have time for calls wherever he was.

It could go on like this for years. Right now, Clint was pretty confident that when the two of them made plans to get together, Jace would show.

One day, he wouldn't. And one day, Clint was sure Jace

would have another man or woman's name on his lips, when Clint couldn't give him the kind of life he wanted.

The last thing Clint wanted to do was hurt Jace. But he never really expected Jace to fall in love. He refused to think about his own goddamned feelings on the subject, because he shouldn't have them.

Now, the emptiness of his apartment nagged at him more than ever. He picked up some catalogs and thought about ordering things like couches and tables, anything beyond the Spartan bed and TV stand he had going on. But hell, he was renting this place, had for the past year, and only now was he thinking that maybe he should own something permanent.

Spies were taught not to do that while they were active in fieldwork. Anyone or anything that you valued too much made you weak, vulnerable, and gave the enemy something to take away from you. Something to hold against you or over you.

Jace was becoming that for Clint, no matter how hard he tried to deny it, and he did. Ignored the lectures that ran, over and over, in his mind. His handlers would tell him to end it.

And his father, well, fuck, he'd broken the rules and then he'd tried to go back and pretend his family didn't exist. Did a great job of it, too.

Goddamn, he hated thinking about his past. He'd pushed it so far back so that he never had to think about it, afraid it would rise up and bite him in the ass at some point.

His father had worked for the CIA. He was what they referred to as a legacy—and, at times, Clint had a lot to live up to. Carl Sommers had been a brilliant man, an even better spy, who'd died doing a job he'd loved more than his family.

There was no other way to say it. And although Clint followed him into the CIA after the military because it was the only kind of life he knew, he never had a true family.

His mom left him and Carl when Clint was thirteen. Fed up with no husband, she met a man who gave her attention, wanted her but not a teenage boy.

"You understand, don't you, Clint?" she'd pleaded, leaving him no choice but to do so. His father had always told him to man up, take over when Carl wasn't around. And Clint did.

It could've turned bad for him in so many ways. Many sons of CIA operatives got themselves in deep trouble. Sometimes it was due to a sense of entitlement or a need for attention from fathers who seemed to give more of it to total strangers than their own families.

Clint had gone the opposite way, studying history and every book ever written on covert ops and the military, and he went that route to get college paid for. He'd applied for Delta to help him learn what his father refused to teach him.

"Be a self-starter, Clint," Carl would boom. All Clint could really remember from those few-days-a-month visits was Carl imbibing too much whiskey and lecturing Clint about shit he had no right to lecture him about. Responsibility.

So Clint held it together all by himself from a too-young age, paid bills, bought groceries, cooked and did laundry, kept up in school as well as keeping up the facade of having a father with him. It entailed staying out of trouble and a lot of creative lying, keeping himself out of anything resembling trouble so as not to get caught. Blowing the ruse would've meant letting down the old man and maybe getting shoved into the foster-care system.

He was a lost boy—Styx called him that once they'd gotten to know each other. There were a lot of them in the CIA, Clint discovered quickly—the wall the job put between them and the rest of the world a perfect way to ensure they'd be great at their jobs and never let real life interfere.

Nature of the game, his friend James used to tell him. *We've got the best of both worlds.*

It was true—as a gay man, a traditional relationship wasn't something he was looking for, and neither were most of the men he'd hooked up with over the years.

Until now.

Goddamned fucking real life in the form of a SEAL named Jace, whose expression when he came was something Clint couldn't erase from his mind.

Maybe you don't want to.

Just the thought of letting someone in made him uneasy. But Jace was getting in, bit by bit, no matter how Clint tried to stop him. It was like Clint never had a chance—and maybe Jace knew it. He was cocky experience and innocence all wrapped up in one tantalizing package.

The ringing phone interrupted his reverie, and he thought back to the last time he'd seen Jack, even as the man called for the third time that week. It had been the night of the explosion when Tomcat died, and he'd planned on celebrating the end of that mission the way he always had—no-strings sex with Jack.

Jack was shorter than Jace, rougher looking but still handsome. Jack had also worked for the CIA for years, and he and Clint had been fucking on and off since the beginning.

It had always been just that for him and for Jack, too, he'd assumed, since they both understood that working for the agency meant no ties.

It was tough watching Jack getting harder after each meeting. Clint used Jack's behavior as a yardstick for himself. He called the man less and less, and when Jack had begun kissing him, he'd remembered why—he'd been with Jace only one weekend, texted back and forth with the boy for months...owed him nothing and still wanted to give him everything.

He'd cursed himself for doing this—for texting Jack in the first place—and yet the explosion had gotten him all twisted up. He'd fucked Jack, and then afterward he pulled away and practically jumped off the damned bed, like he knew he'd done something bad.

"What's wrong?" Jack had asked, still breathing hard from the sex.

"Shit, sorry." He ran a hand along the back of his neck. "The fucking job."

"You know I'm the only one who understands. Come on back to bed and let me help."

"I'm not up for it again. Let's order dinner or something."

"That's cool—I just like spending time with you, Clint. Always have."

Eventually, he'd have to tell Jack the truth. He owed him that. But how could he admit shit to Jack when he couldn't even admit it to himself?

Still, when Jack left that night, Clint knew he'd never let the man back, for sex or anything. Jack had too much poison inside, and as much as it pained Clint to admit it, he was too far gone for anyone to save.

Clint had to concentrate on saving himself. Jace had been slowly yanking him back from the brink, text by text, even fight by fight. The harsh words from the boy were necessary. They'd made him angry, and he was a man who'd never had time for emotions, had pushed them down so often he was sure there were none left.

So yeah, pissed off was good. Jealous was also good. Calling Jace would be even better, if he knew where the boy was.

He didn't want to text or talk to a messaging service. Instead, Clint wrapped a palm around his cock. He was hard all the time now, and he remembered what it had felt like to push inside Jace for the first time, how tight and hot the boy was. How eager.

If he concentrated, he could feel Jace's nails scoring his back when Clint hit his prostate, the surprise of pain turning to pleasure so quickly, the moans ripping from his throat...

Clint was so involved, he nearly ignored the beep of the computer, letting him know someone was trying to Skype with him. But he pulled the computer from the night table, kept it angled at his face in case it was someone he didn't want to see his cock.

Thankfully, it was. Jace came up on the computer screen. His hair was damp, like he'd just showered, and his cheeks were slightly flushed from the sun, the rest of his face tanned. It made his eyes almost glow, and fuck, just seeing him turned Clint on even more.

"Hey, I'm in a hotel till tomorrow," Jace explained. "Nothing to do but sit around."

Seeing Jace nearly made him come, but he held back, gritted his teeth and slowed his roll. Fucking himself watching Jace would be so much more satisfying.

"Glad you got in touch," he managed.

"You sound out of breath. Working out?" Jace asked.

"In a manner of speaking." Clint moved the screen's angle. "I got bored just sitting around."

A pause, and then, "Don't you dare fucking come yet."

Clint watched the blur as Jace stripped onscreen, and then the computer was moved to the bed, its placement giving Clint the maximum view up Jace's body, cock to face.

And it was the boy's face he was most interested in this time.

"Since when do you give the orders?" Clint asked, but his stroking slowed to allow Jace to catch up. Which he did, fast. In moments, Jace was moaning in a low near-growl that sent fire through Clint's blood.

"God, Clint, it's been too long without you."

Jace could say things like that so easily, without a hint of self-consciousness.

Before this, Clint had always held back, scared of leading anyone on. Now, there was no chance of holding back, at least not during this session.

In seconds, Jace's eyes had glazed with the hot lust Clint remembered like it was yesterday. As Clint's fingers wrapped around his cock, his thumb flicked the tip.

Clint touched his tongue to the side of his lips, wished he could reach through the screen and lick him, take him in deep until Jace stiffened and came.

The boy always seemed so surprised when he came hard during their sex. Clint took pride in that.

"Clint, wish you were here," Jace moaned. "Stroking my cock. Pretending it's your hand on my skin."

Staring at the boy like this far exceeded any porn he'd ever seen. Anyone would be lackluster next to the memory of Jace.

Clint looked down as he fisted his weeping cock. "I want you licking my cock. Sucking it. On your knees, looking up at me."

His entire body shuddered as he spoke, remembering, and it was nearly impossible to hold back.

"I'm coming in your mouth, holding your head in place." And then the Dom in him reared his head. "After that, I use

118

heavy, leather-lined cuffs to hold you to the bed. Wrists first and then ankles, so you're spread wide. You can't move—and you love it."

Jace had been silent to that point, but a surprised, sharp intake of breath coupled with a small groan told Clint everything he needed to know. Jace's cheeks were flushed, but he liked the picture Clint painted. Now Clint wouldn't let the boy tear his gaze away as he continued.

"You're begging me to let you go, but I know you don't want that. Your cock's too hard, and when I tweak your nipples with my fingers, you nearly come off the bed. Or you would, if you could. I tell you that I want to spank you. Fuck you. Do anything I want to you and you can't stop me. Would you let me?"

"Yeah. Fuck yeah."

"My cock's inside you, and you're so tight, baby. Chains are clinking while I ride you. You're yelling so loud, like you did the first time I fucked you."

"Clint, I—"

"Don't you dare come yet. That happens when I say."

"Okay."

Clint smiled at the way Jace ground out the word and the frustrated furrow of his brow. "I might let you come when I'm fucking you. Or I might make you wait hours...or days."

"Please..."

"You'll let me turn you over my knee the very next time I see you? You'll walk over to me, climb naked across my lap, bare-assed, and say, 'Spank me, Clint'?"

There was a heated pause, and then Jace spoke, his voice heavy with lust, his blue eyes dark with desire. "You're...serious."

"Very."

"Then yes," Jace told him without a hint of hesitation.

"Good boy. Then come—now."

He watched Jace's orgasm, the visceral moans drifting over him like a caress as Clint shot on his stomach, the climax taking him completely over.

Chapter Fourteen

Two months after their Skype session, Jace walked into his house, his heart hammering. Clint was already there, on Jace's couch, a small smile on his face, like he was enjoying all of Jace's conflicting emotions. But there was true caring behind the smile, coupled with lust.

It helped, marginally. Jace was able to unfist his hands, rub his palms against the rough material of his jungle BDUs. He hadn't even bothered to change when they'd gotten in, just debriefed, gotten a quick okay from the doc and driven home, his hands tight on the wheel, because he knew that no matter what day, what hour, Clint would be here waiting for him. Expecting Jace to make good on his promise, the fantasy that had kept him coming in his sleep for weeks.

You told him you'd do this.

Would Clint leave if Jace couldn't? Jace couldn't see that happening. But they'd been dancing around, getting to know each other for months, and while Jace had known about Clint's kinkier side, he hadn't known Clint could be so commanding. Demanding.

The intensity of the imminent spanking threatened to overwhelm him, and so he stripped his T-shirt, boots and BDUs off. He went to take his tags off but Clint shook his head no.

"I want to hear them jangle," the man explained, and Jace

felt his cheeks grow hot.

Put up or shut up time. And he had a feeling if he put up, the rewards would be huge.

"Trust me, baby," was all Clint said, and Jace moved forward, Clint's words from the phone call echoing in his mind.

You'll let me turn you over my knee the very next time I see you? You'll walk over to me, climb naked across my lap, bare-assed, and say, spank me, Clint?

Telling him without words that he did trust Clint, Jace climbed across the man's lap, and Clint helped him settle in. Jace was vulnerable, exposed, and somehow it was exactly what he needed, and he didn't get the chance to think about just how Clint knew that when the first smack landed hard on his left cheek.

The pause before the second one was the only one he got for what seemed a time measured only in writhing pleasure, hints of pain and the feeling that he was floating, yet he was still secure in the knowledge that Clint would be there to anchor him.

Clint hadn't bothered with commands. Having Jace submit to his fantasy was enough. Waiting to see how responsive he was, the same way Jace had been in his fantasies nightly since the phone call.

His palm delivered a series of blows in no discernible pattern to anyone but him. Jace's ass took on a blushing pink color and then went to bright red as the slaps became more intense. It had been a long time since he'd been with the same man over and over like this, and he knew Jace's hot buttons already. But not all, and the thrill of discovering each and every one kept his cock hard against Jace's belly as the boy cried out.

He could tell that Jace didn't know if he wanted Clint to

stop or not, and that confusion make Clint hold him harder, which in turn made Jace squirm more. Cry out. Curse. And fight like hell once he realized he was going to come from this.

And still Clint continued, calling Jace his sweet virgin baby, telling him how he was going to do this to him every single time he saw him. That maybe he'd take him to a BDSM club and do it in front of people.

When he said that, Jace went taut, and then his body writhed with the intensity of the orgasm.

Clint waited a long moment and then lifted Jace tenderly and cradled him against his chest. "Damn, Jace, you're amazing."

Jace's reply was a soft, contented murmur as he nuzzled Clint harder.

"We're going to have to do that a lot," Clint continued as Jace moaned softly at the thought. "You need it. You want it— and I want to do it for you."

"Jesus, Clint, you're killing me."

"You look cute when you blush," he told Jace, who got angry and in turn blushed harder. "Don't fight me—it's easier to let me have my way with you."

"What else do you want to do to me?" Jace asked, and Clint smiled. "That's a wicked look you've got going on."

"Just remember, you're the one who asked for it."

"It was merely a conversation starter."

"Consider it started. Now I'm going to finish it."

Chapter Fifteen

Rex continued to push him. With every phone call, Sawyer felt his boundaries stretch until he was a taut, turned-on bundle of nerves.

Sex for him had always been good. He'd had regular girlfriends throughout high school and beyond. But he'd been the one in control, a position he generally relished, and he was decidedly uncomfortable and needy all at once in his new role.

By the end of every call, he was hanging on by a thread, waiting for Rex to push him into doing something in person instead of with the phone between them. But Rex never did.

"Is Jace all right?" Rex asked him, right before he hung up. "With Clint, I mean."

"Yeah, I think things are all right. Did you know him from when he was in Delta?"

"We did a couple of joint missions together when he was in Delta," Rex explained. "A few after he got out, too."

Sawyer assumed he was talking about black ops. He knew Rex had a history of coming back from seemingly impossible missions.

"So yeah, the Army and from the clubs."

"Clubs?"

"We were both Doms."

Sawyer almost choked on his tongue, but he tried to play it cool. "Clint was a Dom?"

"He was never full time, but he was more hardcore than I was." There was laughter in Rex's voice, like he knew he'd shocked Sawyer some. "You can ask questions about it, you know."

Since Rex couldn't see the hot flush on his face, Sawyer did. "So you had subs and everything?"

"At one point, I saw some people regularly, yes. Does that bother you?"

"No, the opposite," Sawyer admitted, and Rex laughed.

"I wouldn't mind brushing up on some of my skills, then."

His words made Sawyer shiver. "I wouldn't mind that. If you want."

"Oh, I want. You have no idea how badly I want. It'll give me something nice to dream about. Get some sleep, boy."

Sawyer could barely get out "good night," and when Rex hung up, Sawyer realized that there was no one he'd ever wanted more.

Rex had been a bigger bear than usual while Sawyer had been away, and he'd only gotten worse when Sawyer arrived back, and holy fuck, was Jace the only one who could see the sexual tension between the two of them? Or was it only because he knew Sawyer's feelings—or because Jace was now so caught up in trying to decipher his own?

Now, in the freezing cold surf, the team furiously fought to not get dragged under or freeze to death after half the team had not made time on their earlier run. Sawyer had improved his time dramatically—which was something, considering he'd

SE Jakes

already been the fastest—and still Rex singled him out.

And he knew they'd all pay during training.

"What's up his ass?" Jace muttered.

"I'll tell you later," Sawyer said, and Jace agreed because they were literally about to drown. While they'd kept in touch, Sawyer mainly wanted to hear about things with Clint and hadn't mentioned any Rex drama.

Four hours later, waterlogged but dry, Jace waited on Sawyer, having grabbed both of them lunch.

"And don't come back until you remember how we do things around here!" Rex roared as minutes later, Sawyer slammed into the private mess the SEAL team used. Thankfully, Jace was the only one to hear the yelling, but Sawyer was oddly not as pissed or embarrassed as he normally was.

He looked—confused, almost. And it didn't take much for him to spill about the phone calls.

"Phone sex," he clarified around a mouthful of sandwich.

"You called him?"

"Other way around."

Jace raised his brows. "That's a start."

"I'm a fucking coward," Sawyer muttered. "You don't have to rub it in."

"I'm not pushing you. When it happens, it happens."

Sawyer snorted, and Jace continued, "You'd think that the yelling would've improved. He's almost worse."

"I know. It's almost like he's pissed that he even has feelings for me."

"Any idea why?"

"None." Sawyer sat back and glanced around the busy

126

mess hall. His friend got hit on as much, if not more so than Jace himself by women and men. He had a similar look to Jace's, although Sawyer's hair was darker, but Sawyer's face held a harder edge.

Dammit, he didn't like to watch the guy in pain.

He shifted in his seat, as his ass had finally unfrozen and was beginning to sting again from the spanking and the various other ways Clint finished him last night, and he tried not to wince.

"Clint around?"

"Yeah, he's around, all right." It was Jace's turn to mutter.

"So things are good, then?" Sawyer asked as Jace took a bite of his sandwich, suddenly starving.

"It's just...time."

Sawyer pulled his brows together as Jace struggled to explain further. "It's like, trying to make this happen...every time we get together we have to learn about each other all over again."

"Hell, I see Rex daily and I still can't pull my shit together," Sawyer pointed out. "Maybe you say it's time because you're not ready to admit that you want more."

Jace nodded, not wanting to delve into the truth of his friend's words just yet, so he changed the subject. "You and Rex... Gonna step that up anytime soon?"

"Fuck you."

Jace grinned. "Clint knows Rex. I guess Rex made some calls after I thought Clint was killed."

"Yeah. I'm friends with this guy, Tanner—he's Delta. The guy he's with is friends with Rex and Clint, too. I guess they all met when they were Doms."

Jace almost choked on his next bite of sandwich, more

acutely aware of his tanned hide than ever. Sawyer looked heartily amused that his friend hadn't known that Clint had been a Dom.

"I'm going to strangle you," Jace managed.

"Don't act like he hasn't tried stuff on you," Sawyer said, then leaned in. "Has he?"

"No comment." Fuck, why hadn't Clint told him? Sure, Jace liked the commands and being tied down, but hell, the Dom thing took it to another level.

Why hadn't he mentioned it?

"If you're into that sort of thing, more power to you," Sawyer said. "It gave me some food for thought."

"You asked about him?"

"Figured you might want some more info." Sawyer smiled, and Jace shook his head. He caught a glimpse of Rex in the corner, talking to another captain, and, as usual, Rex's eyes strayed toward Sawyer. It was like the guy had a beacon that went directly to the younger SEAL, and Jace wondered when the two of them would finally do something about the attraction.

But Sawyer was still hard-pressed to be convinced that he should move on his feelings, and Jace's mind was swimming with the fact that Clint had been a Dom.

"Come on, we've got a full afternoon of training to go," he told Sawyer, and the men finished their lunches and headed out for another afternoon of pain.

Chapter Sixteen

Jace slammed in and threw his bag halfway across the room. He hadn't wanted what Sawyer had so innocently told him to get to him so badly, but fuck, it just emphasized how little he and Clint really did know about each other.

A Dom...hell, that was a big part of someone's life. Why hadn't Clint mentioned it? Or was what he did to Jace considered Domming? Was Clint looking at him as a sub or a lover? Or something more, which was really what Jace wanted.

"This relationship shit sucks balls," he muttered. He hesitated with the phone in his hand as to whether or not he should call when he was this pissed off and decided he couldn't sit around brooding about it all goddamned night. He had training at o-dark-hundred.

Clint answered on the fourth ring. It sounded like he was in a bar—or a club or who the hell knew when he said, "Hey, what's up?"

Ah, fuck it. "I don't want to bother you if you're out."

"It's not a bother."

"Just call me back when you can talk, all right?"

"What's the problem, Jace?" Clint asked, and suddenly there was no other background noise, so the man had obviously gone outside or someplace else, and that made Jace feel marginally better.

Jace took a deep breath and dove in. "When were you going to tell me you were a Dom?"

Clint paused for a long moment and then asked, "Who's talking to you about my sexual preferences?"

"Someone who knows you a hell of a lot better than me, obviously," Jace muttered. "So I'm guessing it's true."

"Okay, yes, I'm technically a Dom but—"

"But what? You're Domming me without me knowing it?"

"I didn't really think about it like that, but hell, you seem to be enjoying it," Clint said.

"This isn't funny. Is that all I am to you—someone to play with?"

"We've had this discussion."

"We really haven't, Clint. And I didn't feel like having it now."

"Then why did you call?"

"Because I'm fucking pissed off. Look, I've gotta go."

"Always need to get your way."

"I could say the same thing about you."

"Grow the hell up, Jace." And Clint hung up before he had a chance to.

Six hours later, Jace was staring at the ceiling when the phone rang. He turned it over in his palm, thought about not picking up, but what would that solve?

"Hey," he said.

"Hey." Clint cleared his throat. "I'm not running around playing Dom with anyone, okay? I haven't done that lifestyle for

130

a long time, but I do like aspects of it. If I'd thought it was important to tell you, if I thought it would impact us, I would've shared, all right?"

"I guess neither of us is used to sharing anything," Jace said.

"We don't have to—"

"Do Dom stuff?" Jace asked, a smile on his lips before he could stop it. "I didn't say I minded. I just don't like being caught off guard."

"Understood."

"How into it were you?"

"Every chance I got."

"So you did...everything?"

"Want me to spell it out?"

"I think I do." Jace got comfortable even as his cock hardened.

"What are you picturing?"

Jace laughed a little. "You. Leather. Bare chest. A whip."

"You're not far off."

"Jesus."

"If I'd met you in the club...a real, live virgin in every sense of the BDSM world...holy hell, Jace, you would've been in trouble."

"Good trouble?"

"Based on your definition, I believe so." Clint paused. "Jace, the Dom thing...I never meant to...I mean, I'm not looking for a full-time D/s thing. I just really like rough fucking. Ropes, cuffs..."

"Spankings."

"Yeah, lots of that."

"Me too," Jace admitted. "It helps, somehow."

"It helps me, too. I never thought to tell you because it's just a part of who I am. I don't go to the clubs anymore. I stopped that a while ago. I always thought I had your consent to do what we've been doing, but if that's not the way you feel, tell me. Because I thought the sex was pretty damned hot. Keeps me coming back."

Jace wasn't sure why those last words made him tense up, but they did. To have come this far—or what he'd assumed was this far—and hear that was worse than a physical blow.

Instead of telling Clint that, he said, "You have my consent." *To fuck me. To break my goddamned heart. To do anything you want to me.*

Clint had from the beginning.

Chapter Seventeen

Jace's calf was bleeding, and he was pretty sure there was blood mixed in with the sweat in his boots. All his body wanted to do was collapse onto the double bed, because it was cool and clean in the hotel room, and soon enough he'd be back out in the fray when the intel got clearance or some such shit.

Because of the threats made to the FOB, the military PTB had decided that hiding the SEALs was safest. They'd had far too many losses in recent months, and they'd gotten smarter.

He pulled his shirt off as he noticed the tub, separate from the stall shower. Very American and very welcome so he could get clean and soak away some aches—two birds, one stone. All in all, he'd been OUTCONUS for three months, with no end in sight.

Well, there was *supposed* to be a light at the end of that tunnel tonight, because Clint was set to meet him here. He hadn't told the man where he was, but Clint had his sources, and they were supposed to catch up in the hotel at some point this week.

But Jace knew that he needed to cancel Clint's visit, because the man didn't need to deal with his shit. Jace still didn't know what end of the Dom situation was up, and he knew Clint came to him for relaxation, not stress. Jace still hadn't gotten past the Dom stuff, even though he'd been reluctant to bring it up again.

I thought the sex was pretty damned hot. Keeps me coming back.

Jace pushed down that sentence he'd been replaying over and over in his mind since their last call and sent his text canceling their meeting. Hell, he didn't even know if Clint was close or still in the States, so maybe it didn't matter.

But after he sent the text, his stomach dropped. He hadn't realized how much he'd been looking forward to seeing Clint, to hoping he could get past hearing those words over and over in his mind. Sure, he liked the sex—loved it—but somewhere along the way, he'd known he needed more. And now, after months of thinking Clint might need more as well, he was now convinced that Clint didn't.

He slept away most of the day and the night, and when he got up, he didn't even know or care what time it was. He still felt like shit physically, and so he finally took the painkillers Doc gave him. And then he set about filling the tub as he stripped, and then he washed the dirt off in the shower before getting out and sinking into the clean, warm water in the tub, letting it work some of the kinks out.

He wasn't going to feel human for a long while. He leaned his head back, closed his eyes and felt the room spin.

"Fuck." Not good. But he'd refused to stay in the hospital, and the doc had said the concussion was mild.

Didn't feel that way. And maybe the tub hadn't been the best of ideas.

He hadn't expected the painkillers to kick in that quickly. Drugs had always affected him too easily, which was why he rarely took anything stronger than OTC stuff. But Doc had insisted because of his ribs and other various and sundry injuries, including the pounding head.

He grabbed the towel bar that he wasn't really sure would hold him up as a wave of dizziness hit. Cursed, made a foggy mental note to never take painkillers again right before he saw Clint in the bathroom, grabbing for him.

If Clint hadn't been there to catch him, Jace would've gone down hard. As it was, Clint had a tough time with the slippery, naked body, but he managed. Held Jace under his arms as the boy insisted he was fine.

Jace looked up at him, his eyes dulled from painkillers, his voice slurred. "How the hell did you get in here?"

"If you seriously think a locked hotel door's going to stop me, you're more drugged than I thought." He moved forward, because Jace looked really unsteady. "Come on, let's get you back to bed."

"I'm not an invalid."

Clint ignored the mumblings, because he would've been doing the same thing.

"I've got it. Don't need help," Jace insisted as he tried to get his legs untangled from the tub. Finally, Clint lifted him out completely and placed him securely out of the bathroom and onto the rug in the main room.

"Yeah, you really looked like you had it," Clint told him. "Don't be stubborn."

"Can't rely on you like this."

Clint knew what Jace meant, but it was still a punch in the gut. "You would've caught yourself if I wasn't here," he lied to the boy, which mollified him enough to stop resisting Clint's hands on him.

"Bullshit, and you know it. Fucking painkillers."

Clint snorted. "Stay right here."

He reached into the bathroom, taking his hands off Jace for only a moment before returning with a towel. He dried the boy off before lowering him into the bed, taking care with the cuts and bruises he saw. Jace's feet were particularly bad, and Clint would wait until Jace stopped saying he could take care of everything, and then Clint *would* take care of everything.

Jace muttered something about doing it himself, and while Clint ignored him in favor of getting him comfortable, Jace finally lost his battle against the painkillers.

As he watched over the boy, the text message he'd sent ran over and over in Clint's mind—*Not feeling up to sex—don't bother making the trip.* And he didn't know how to take that. Jace had been in his life for over a year now and didn't think Clint wanted anything more from him than sex, and how had that happened?

Granted, the sex was good. Hot as hell, but he liked spending time with Jace, too. That's why he always booked multiple nights at the hotels he'd meet the boy at in between missions instead of just popping in for a single night here and there.

You've never told him, though.

And as soon as he'd realized that, he'd shoved his clothes into a bag and prepared to close the distance between them more quickly than he'd planned on. Literally and figuratively.

He thought back on their previous conversations, knew the Dom thing had thrown Jace, and maybe that had something to do with all of this. As he contemplated, he woke the boy up every half an hour for the next three hours—each time, Jace either cursed or gave him the finger—and that seemed to really be the only sleep the kid needed.

His eyes looked clearer, and his stomach growled. He propped himself up, still in obvious pain.

"Want to eat in bed?"

"Sure. You didn't—"

"Have to do this? I know." He pushed a tray to Jace's lap. "There are a lot of things I do because I want to."

Jace stared up at him, an understanding in his eyes. He ate seconds and thirds, took more pain pills at Clint's insistence and then lay back down.

This time, Clint joined him in the bed. Massaged every part of his aching body, ending with a back rub. He kneaded Jace's muscles until Jace melted into the bed. The kid groaned his contentment, then practically purred into the pillow.

"Glad you're feeling better."

"Guess you're waiting for an apology."

"Don't need one."

Jace peered over his shoulder. "What do you need? Because I'm not exactly up to much."

"Jesus, what did I do to make you think the only thing I want from you is sex? If you think I'd expect you to perform right now in the condition you're in... Fuck, I just wanted to hold you."

And maybe he could sound like more of a girl. A lovesick one at that. But still, he pulled Jace to him gently, stroked the man's hair.

"I didn't know—didn't think that you..." Jace stopped to collect himself. "It's not that I don't want you to want me for more than sex, but—"

"But I guess I'm better at hiding my feelings than I thought."

"I thought—"

"Well, keep thinking more. Because there is more, all right?" Clint said fiercely.

"You're pissed."

"At myself, for letting you think all this time I've only come to you for a fuck. Don't get me wrong—that's hot. It's more than most guys have. But I thought...you mean more to me than that. Maybe it's all you want, but I want you to know this is more for me. So when you texted and told me not to come because you were not up to it...I didn't know what to think."

"And you came anyway."

Chapter Eighteen

Jace stared at him, a look of obvious surprise on his face at Clint's admission. "I guess I didn't think you'd want to deal with this."

"With what? Real life?" Clint pulled him closer. "I think you're the one who doesn't want that put on him. But hey, I didn't mean to freak you out."

"Oh, fuck you." Jace started to tug away, and Clint pulled him back hard. But Jace fought him with a surprising strength. "It's not like I know shit about you."

"What are you talking about? Christ, we talked about this last time—I'm with you, Jace. Just you."

"On your terms. It's always you—always up to you," Jace pointed out. "Your schedule, you coming to me. Do you realize I don't even know where you fucking live now?"

Clint blinked. "I haven't told anyone that in a long time."

"Because of the CIA?"

"Because I never had the reason to."

"Guess you still don't." Jace shoved him away hard, hands to his chest, but Clint didn't fall back, only because of his training. But most would have—Jace was strong as anything, and right now spitting mad, despite his injuries.

Can you blame him?

He wanted to answer yes but in good conscience couldn't. "Look, that's your assumption—it's not how I feel. It was—"

"What, an oversight? For a year?" Jace gave a short laugh as he stood, but there was absolutely no mirth behind it.

Clint joined him to put an end to it then and there, grabbed Jace and put him back on the bed, and despite the struggle, managed to do it with a minimum of Jace hurting himself.

But he still was breathing hard, holding his ribs.

"Asshole," he puffed at Clint.

"Okay, yeah, I deserved that, but I'm fucking here, right?" Clint demanded. "I'm here, for you. Again. You push me away and I still come. I've never done that before, with anyone. Not in thirty-six years."

"Your headstone said thirty-seven."

"They were wrong!" he roared.

"Didn't realize you were touchy about your age."

"Are you deliberately trying to antagonize me?"

Jace shrugged a little, then winced. "Misery loves company."

Clint softened, took Jace's face in his hand. "I'll take your company any way I can get it."

Jace closed his eyes tightly and turned his head away. Clint lay next to him and just held him for a while before adding, "I didn't mean to forget that this is all new to you too."

Jace stiffened a little, his face buried to Clint's shoulder. "Drives me fucking nuts."

"I think relationships are supposed to do that."

"Christ," Jace muttered, "just fuck me before I grow girl parts, okay?"

"Happy to oblige. But you lie there and let me do all the

work."

"Girl parts," Jace reminded him. "I'm participating or it's not happening."

"Stubborn jackass." Clint told him, but he didn't prevent Jace from trying to do what he could, pain and all.

Clint would just need to make sure that the pleasure overrode the pain.

"You going to make it all better with sex?" Jace asked.

"Yes," Clint answered simply, and Jace laughed, a real one, and he didn't protest when Clint pushed him back and kissed him, their tongues dueling.

At first Jace didn't fight his position. No, in fact he spread his legs and cocked one around Clint's thigh, seemed content that their bodies were close, their erections rubbing against each other.

But after that, there was no fantasy here—no gentling. It was rough and tumble, and Jace fought him every step of the way. Clint knew Jace was looking for an apology—that he was angry and hurt even after the sex, and maybe he didn't even know exactly why.

But Clint knew there was something he could do to help. While Jace lay there, Clint went and found his phone.

"What are you doing?"

"Putting my address in your phone."

"Clint, look, I didn't mean to make a big deal out of it," Jace started.

"We've been sleeping together for over a year and you don't know where I live. I think maybe you're right to make a big deal out of it," Clint told him.

Clint's gesture meant more to Jace than Clint could

possibly know. It also gave Jace the impetus to let Clint in on what was really bothering him. "You're always there for me. I have to look at your actions. And I was, but then...you said the sex is what kept you coming back."

"What?"

"When we were talking about the Dom stuff."

Clint came back to the bed, ran a hand down the side of Jace's neck, then cupped the back of it. "Sex isn't what keeps me coming back. It never has with anyone else. But the sex we have...it's more than sex. It's a connection. You have to know that."

"I guess I did, on some level."

"I don't want you to ever think that I want anything from you but you."

Jace believed him and still... "I don't know if it's enough anymore, the way things are."

He held his breath as Clint studied him, tried to keep his expression neutral, like Clint's answer wouldn't matter much, but judging by the look in Clint's eyes, Jace had failed miserably at that. "You know what, forget it—I don't want to force—"

"You wouldn't be forcing anything, Jace," Clint said quietly. "If you really want...more, for us...well, I think we're already there. You're just the first one with the balls to admit it."

"So what, we just keep going the way we're going, seeing each other every few months?"

"For you, I'd be willing to change that."

"Holy fuck."

Clint laughed as the words slipped out of Jace's mouth.

"Am I in that alone?" he asked, and Jace could only shake his head no and Clint smiled.

Since he'd told Clint to stay away tonight and the man had come anyway, his presence alone would've been enough to comfort Jace, but the conversation was better than anything he could've hoped for. He didn't want to push his luck, so he rubbed his body against Clint's. "Fuck, how do you always manage to make me hard?"

"A talent," Clint said, reaching out to stroke him. "You're going to come, then sleep, then not worry about anything."

And just like that, they'd gone to a new level, and Jace was vulnerable and new to all of this, trusting himself and trusting Clint. But he let himself stop thinking, felt boneless when Clint touched him. The painkillers were working now, but he was past the point of caring how drugged-up he was. The fight was over, but watching Clint hovering over him, his stomach flipped like he was a damned virgin again.

Clint stroked his face. "It's okay, baby. I know."

He wanted to ask how the man knew, but what would it matter? He believed him, trusted him. But still, he trembled as Clint moved between his legs—part nervousness, part shyness—and spread them wide, holding them apart with his own thighs. There was nothing Jace could do but enjoy Clint's machinations.

"Put your hands by your sides and keep them there."

Jace hesitated for just a second, and Clint continued casually, "Unless you'd rather I use my handcuffs."

Jace's cock jumped even as he put his hands to fist the sheets by his thighs. Clint gave a short laugh, but he wasn't laughing at him at all.

"Good boy. Just relax," Clint told him. "It'll happen naturally, if you let it. And this way you won't hurt yourself. I want you still. I'll do all the work."

Once Clint explained his reasoning, Jace felt a little better.

143

He leaned his head back as Clint began to suckle his balls, taking one, then the other into his mouth, and the sensation was mind-blowing, especially when Clint tugged on Jace's dick in tandem with it. His cock leaked, his breath was quicker now and he kept his hands behind his head, fingers locked, the way Clint wanted it.

He wasn't sure why that was so damned hot, but it was.

And then Clint was finger-fucking his ass and sucking his dick, and Jace couldn't do much but buck up every once in a while, and Clint even found a way to foil that small movement without ever stopping what he was doing. And Jesus, it felt good, and Jace realized he was moaning and trying to say something—anything—all of it pretty much incomprehensible.

But when he came, in a spurting rush in Clint's mouth, he heard the words *I love you* echoing inside his head and prayed to fucking God he didn't say them out loud. Because Clint would think he was some stupid sap who mistook lust for love.

Except...he never had before.

During an orgasm wasn't the time to say it—even he knew that. He'd been forced to sit through enough chick flicks to know.

"You all right?" Clint murmured as he wiped Jace's brow. There was sweat covering his entire body, like he'd just come back from a long-distance run, and his heart was beating like crazy.

"Great," he managed. "Really fucking great."

Sawyer knew Rex was in the next room. If he put the phone on mute, he'd probably hear the man through the door that connected the rooms, and somehow, that made it hotter.

He'd been waiting for the call, staring at the phone most of the night and wondering what Rex would make him talk about tonight.

He's not making you do anything.

In fact, Sawyer was enjoying Rex's seduction, had no doubt that was exactly what it was. It had been unexpected and hot as anything the first time, and he knew there would be more to come. And the calls happened pretty regularly, each time leaving Sawyer to wonder what would happen if he drove to Rex's house and just went inside. But he never did.

But all of this was fantasy, and Sawyer was thinking of something far deeper—because he knew he loved the goddamned man. Knew it the way he knew he'd be a good SEAL, the way he knew just the right shot to take.

He knew it because it was as easy as breathing. He wanted to sit and listen to the man tell his stories forever—at times, when Rex let his guard down in the group and talked, Sawyer pretended Rex was just talking to him, that it was only the two of them at the table, drinking beers and then going home together.

Man, he was so turned around.

It could happen, Sawyer.

But there was still Rex's past to consider, and living in someone else's shadow, well, that was something he couldn't handle. And phone calls weren't real life.

And still, he hung on to the phone like it was his lifeline.

Finally, just before he drifted to sleep, his phone rang.

"You doing okay?" Rex asked. His voice was hoarse, and he didn't sound like his usual self when he made these calls.

"Yeah, I'm good."

"I woke you."

SE Jakes

"Almost, but it's okay." He paused. "You don't sound okay."

"I'm not," Rex admitted, and there was a long silence until he said, "Talking to you helps."

Sawyer smiled into the phone. "Nice to hear. I was beginning to feel selfish, because you always help me."

"It always helps me, too, boy. I don't mind taking care of you. I like it. Like that you can let your guard down in front of me."

Sawyer took a deep breath and asked the question he needed to before the sex talk started. "Have you ever been in love?"

"Yes," Rex admitted gruffly, and Sawyer decided not to push that right now. The fact that he wasn't hiding it was a good thing.

"Do you think it's weird that we're doing this over the phone instead of face to face?"

"No."

"If I was there, with you, what would you do?" He held his breath, because typically it was Rex leading the call, asking for Sawyer's fantasy.

But Rex didn't seem to care about that.

"I wouldn't have stopped that night in the alley," his CO told him, and Sawyer caught his cock in his hand before Rex got the next words out. Closed his eyes and let the words bring him into the fantasy. "If you'd told me that you wanted me, I would've kissed you until you couldn't see straight. I can still feel your cock pressed against me—you were so hard, so worried I'd feel it. So worried you didn't notice I was harder."

Sawyer let his finger play along the tip of his cock, pretending it was Rex's tongue as the man continued, "I would've gotten on my knees, wouldn't care that anyone could

146

walk out and see us. Would've swallowed your cock and watched you, half panic, half pleasure, not sure which one would win out."

"Pleasure," Sawyer managed, because he was in that alley now, his cock in Rex's mouth, the threat of being caught imminent, and he just didn't care.

"But that's not what I fantasize about most," Rex admitted. "I can't stop thinking about the first time you walked into my office. Yelling. The look on your face when you realized it wasn't your old CO...I want to freeze that moment in time."

"What would you have done?"

Rex laughed, a wicked sound, and Sawyer's entire body heated. "I would've ordered you to turn around and lock the door. In my fantasy, you do it, but you look nervous, like you know what's coming. And then I tell you that you need some discipline. A lot of it, and all of it would come from me from that point on. And you have no choice but to agree."

Sawyer closed his eyes, let Rex's voice bring him right back to his office.

"The first thing I do is reach across the desk and yank you over it. Your face is in line with my crotch. I make you open my pants with your teeth and you do it, and when my cock comes out, I tell you to suck on it. And you do. You're looking up at me and you're sucking. And you're scared that someone's going to come in. And I tell you, don't worry—this is nothing. I'm going to have your pants down and you bent over my desk before the afternoon is over."

That was all it took—Sawyer shot with a loud groan, helpless to stop himself. When he could talk, he said, "Sorry."

"I couldn't have held out much longer myself. Jesus."

"Remember where you left off on that, please."

Rex snorted. Typically, this was where Rex signed off, when they were both semi-satisfied and ready for sleep. But this time, even though they lay in separate beds in separate rooms as always, this was the closest Sawyer ever felt to the man, and neither one was ready to end the conversation.

Chapter Nineteen

Clint slept. Jace watched his profile, wondered when was the last time Clint had actually done so.

Jace knew from experience that you could only go so long without. Most special-forces types—and CIA types—rarely let their guards down enough to get comfortable enough to do so in someone else's presence. The fact that Clint had erased some of Jace's embarrassment at being taken care of earlier.

He'd let Clint take care of him physically, but allowing him in emotionally was a much harder proposition. For Clint, too, he supposed, since the man never spoke of his past or much about his job, unless they were comparing the various shitholes they'd had the pleasure of fighting for their country in.

Truth be told, getting taken care of physically was probably harder for Jace than the emotional crap. But who was he kidding—all of this was new to him.

He moved restlessly, the painkillers still dimming enough of his injuries that he was feeling good—albeit a little high. He finished more of the food Clint had ordered, hit the head and then checked his messages.

Still no news, which, for him, was good. Meant more time in the hotel with Clint. And two hours of sleep were more than enough for him.

Executive decision made, he pushed the covers aside and

slid between the man's legs. Nuzzled his cock before swallowing half of it and felt Clint wake up with a jerk and a curse, followed quickly by a moan.

"Christ, Jace, why don't you let me take care of you? You're the one who's hurt."

Jace let him slip from his mouth only long enough to say, "You already did that."

Clint gave a sleepy grin and brushed hair from Jace's eyes as he went back to work, licking and laving Clint's thick cock, his hands spreading the man's thighs so he could have full access to his balls as well.

"Jesus, Jace." Clint took them into his mouth, one by one, suckling with enough pressure to make the man jump. He laughed, knowing it would vibrate up with a jolt through Clint. Knowing it—and everything else—would drive him crazy.

Finally, he decided to end Clint's suffering, sucked him in deep as he stroked. Clint moved his hips in time with Jace's rhythm—wouldn't last, and it didn't matter.

Their sex wasn't rushed. They didn't need to make anything quick, as they had at least forty-eight hours and a hotel room and nothing else to do but each other.

With every hour that passed, Jace's body became less sore. He'd been trained to recover quickly, to ignore pain, to take rest when needed, and his body responded to everything Clint did.

He realized that a lot of his problem was the guilt he harbored over Kenny and the deal with the Feds. Until he got that under control, then he'd always be walking on eggshells.

He felt like a traitor, even though he'd done nothing wrong. He wasn't hurting Clint's job as Tomcat, because Clint was out and safe, and the Feds weren't doing anything with the intel Jace had given them.

And Kenny continued to get in deeper with the MC even as Jace was dug in up to his neck with the Feds. The best he could do was keep the information he gave the Feds as brief as possible and try to convince Kenny to get the hell out of town. And if that didn't happen...well, he'd eventually have to ask for Clint's help in getting the Feds to cut him loose without getting either of them in deep shit.

"What's wrong?" Clint asked him now, and Jace tried to explain, "It's all so fucking fragile."

"Always is. That's why we have to make the most of it."

Rex talked about the current mission for a few minutes. About the hotel security. About anything but what he really wanted to talk to Sawyer about.

The boy didn't push it, let Rex work up to it, and Rex was grateful. It allowed him to finally open up to Sawyer about his imprisonment.

"I was thinking about the capture tonight. Most of the time, I can push it back, but sometimes it surprises me. Better to talk about it than to let fear take root." Rex paused and then, "You asked before if I'd ever been in love. His name was Josh. And I couldn't save him. I wanted to, but I know now there was nothing I could do. He'd have told me the same thing."

"He was a SEAL?"

"Yes."

"You were captured with him."

"I was." Rex willed himself not to hang up, because dealing with this was the only way to keep moving. "We were together for four years. Worked together. No one knew we were together. It didn't affect our jobs. If anything, I thought it made me better. And I've been pushing you away because...maybe this isn't fair to you. Maybe I'm not the right guy for you."

"Never thought any guy was right for me," Sawyer said. "That's part of the problem. But when I saw you, after I'd yelled at you..."

"Yeah, I know." The sight of the young SEAL, so serious and so damned handsome, standing across from him, detailing the problems the team was having with leadership, had made Rex want to drag him into his lap.

It had been the first time anyone caught his interest like that since Josh, and it had surprised him and made him get pissed at Sawyer for no good reason, like it had somehow been his fault.

"You knew I fell for you?"

"Not at first, but after while, well, let's just say you didn't hide it well," Rex said, and Sawyer laughed a little.

"I was pretty stunned. After what happened with Josh, you still want to start something with another military man? I mean—the same risks apply."

"I know. I've tried to go the other way, but safe doesn't suit me. Never did. And I figure no risk, no reward." Rex paused. "I've been waiting a long time for someone like you—I won't throw it away because there's danger involved."

It all made so much sense now—Rex pushed all of them hard—Sawyer maybe more—but the reasons were embedded in his flesh. Sawyer had seen the scars on the man's back, and they made Rex even more attractive to him.

"Don't hang up yet," Sawyer said. "I wanted to tell you about another fantasy I had."

Rex got hard, despite the emotion of the call, or maybe because of it. "I'm listening."

Chapter Twenty

Clint spent four days with Jace in the hotel. On their last night, they had a huge fight about Jace still being involved in the MC, and they hadn't recovered from it when it was time for Jace to move out into the mission again.

After that, Jace's mission was four months of pure fucking hell. Whatever could go wrong, did. Rex spent the entire time pissed, and Sawyer tried to fix everything, and there was nothing the SEALs could've done differently.

Jace was doing all right, holding it together, and he thought, all in all, they pulled off a damned good op. It was after hearing about the explosions that he'd gone numb.

A helo sent to rescue troops was shot down by rebels outside the mountains of Afghanistan, resulting in the deaths of six SEALs. Jace's team had been nowhere near it, but they were supposed to have been the ones on the helo that morning. Circumstances beyond their control had trapped them inside their current FOB. That guilt was compounded by the fact that they knew most of those men who died, and so the loss weighed heavily on all of them. He'd worked with those men before—they were from the Coronado teams, and some he'd gone through early BUD/s training with.

He pulled himself together enough to be allowed home, knowing he'd have to go back and see the military shrink before being cleared for duty, because no one bounced back from shit like this, no matter how strong they purported to be. But he didn't have to deal with that now.

He was finally home, alone, trying to come down from the entire trip. His packs sat in the front hallway, and he'd stripped and climbed into the walk-in shower with a bottle of whiskey, sat on the floor and just let the heat and alcohol mix.

Six men gone. Six families left to mourn. The media was having a field day, although they'd never know all the details about the deaths of his fellow SEALs and other members of the special forces community. But Jace knew, in more detail than he ever cared to.

How was he supposed to handle it?

You just will.

He thought about calling Clint, who'd no doubt heard the news by now, but he didn't think he knew how to share shit like this, let alone deal with it for himself. Clint would make him deal with it without dealing with them. After four months of not speaking beyond texts, they were strangers again, strangers who knew each other sexually better than a lot of couples.

Jace didn't want the stranger—he wanted Clint.

He felt so fucking empty inside, and he couldn't even bring himself to go to the bar where some of the other men were, celebrating their fallen. Jace didn't know if he was having trouble facing his own mortality or if the stuff with the MC was weighing too heavily on him to handle it the way he might normally have, but the fact that good men died with no way to fight back was too much for him to handle.

And it could've been him. Things had gone from celebratory to horrible in the space of a week, and there was a hole within the teams that would be impossible to fill. New SEALs would come in, but they wouldn't be the same.

The shower door opened, and Clint was there, with way too much pity in his eyes for Jace to handle.

"Thanks for letting me know you were alive," were the first words out of his mouth.

Fuck. He'd just assumed Clint would know. "Sorry," he managed before the man dragged him from under the now-cold spray and wrapped him in a towel.

The whiskey hadn't done enough damage, in Jace's estimation, since he was still able to think and reason, and he hated that. Hated the betrayed look that fought for space in Clint's expression more. "You don't have to stay."

"The hell I don't." Clint's voice was low, although that didn't mean he wasn't angry. But Jace was—really fucking angry at everyone and everything, and he stumbled past Clint and got into bed, still damp. Clint had confiscated his bottle, but the bed and his life were already spinning.

Clint watched Jace shove himself under the covers. "I'm guessing you don't want to talk about it—but you should."

"Now you're my shrink?" Jace turned his back to Clint and pulled the blanket over him like they were complete fucking strangers, and Clint fought the urge to kick the shit out of him and make him talk.

Because Clint would be the same exact way were he in Jace's position. And he had been, literally, so many times during Delta especially, when he worked with a close-knit team and everyone knew everyone and every damned thing, every single death was so personal it burned like hot metal in his mouth. It was when every mission began to feel like revenge that he knew it was time to get out.

Revenge was never good for the person seeking it. In the end, it always came back to bite you on the ass.

Jace hadn't moved. Wasn't sleeping and didn't even have the nerve to pretend he was. So Clint took his shoulder and pushed him to his back.

Jace stared up at him and said, "What?" and then rolled his eyes.

"Don't make me pull this out of you."

"Leave it alone. Christ, this is part of why I didn't call. You don't have to put me back together, dammit—that's not your responsibility."

"And if I make it mine?"

"It's not."

"Stubborn son of a bitch." Clint pinned him to the bed, enjoyed watching him struggle under his grasp. "I want to be here for all of it. That's why I came to 'Stan for you. That's why I'm here."

"To make me talk about things better left unsaid."

"Trust me, they're not." Clint kept a hand wound around Jace's wrists even as he reached for the handcuffs.

Jace struggled, but his dick hardened against Clint's. "Just stop talking and fuck me, okay? That's what we do well."

"I told you, that's not why I'm here. Not why I come to you."

"Then what's all this about?" Jace was furious now, jerking his wrists apart like he could break the cuffs, and if Clint gave him any amount of time, drunk or not, Jace would get out of them.

Instead, he pulled the naked man forward, forcing him to come to a rest over his knees.

"Clint—don't."

"Afraid you won't like it? Or are you afraid you will?"

Jace answered by trying to buck away, which was

impossible. And Clint knew this could provide the best release possible for him, even though he'd fight it all the way.

He ran a hand over the boy's bare ass, which was smooth and begged to be reddened. The Dom in him reared his head, and he ran a cool hand over the warm flesh, heard Jace begin to whimper his plea, as if that might get him off the hook.

It made Clint hard to hear it, though, the soft words that Jace muttered. He continued to rub, letting the boy think he might possibly be relenting.

He might not Dom on a regular basis any longer, but he was damned good at it—and he planned on letting Jace get the benefits of his expertise tonight. Because this would be nothing like the first time.

Chapter Twenty-One

Clint was rubbing his ass, and Jace was pretty sure he'd never felt—or been—more vulnerable in his entire life. It was completely different from the first time, because then Jace had come to him willingly. Had been in a hell of a good state of mind.

How he'd gotten into this position, he still wasn't sure, but he was sure this wasn't Clint's first time restraining someone to do this. It made him almost want to go through with it in order to wipe away memories of other men across Clint's lap, to blow them out of the water, to make Clint want no one but him.

On the other hand, the vulnerability wasn't something he was used to or liked in the least bit. His emotions were too damned close to the surface—one stroke and he knew he'd be breaking apart. He wasn't naive, knew what Clint was doing even though he'd never thought he'd be in this position.

"You've done this a lot."

"You want to talk about the Dom thing again?"

"Yeah, *talk* being the operative word."

"Sorry, we're past that," Clint told him. "You can talk. I'll be doing other things."

"I'm not your fucking sub."

"Did you want to be?" Clint asked mildly. "You're jealous of the other men who've been stretched across my lap, begging for my hand."

Jace gritted his teeth and tried for escape one last time. "Clint, I'll talk to you, okay? Just let me up."

"Sure, baby." Clint's voice was rough with lust as his hand rubbed the crack of Jace's ass. "Is that what you really want?"

"Yes."

"This is what I want." Clint's hand smacked down hard on his ass before Jace had a chance to draw his next breath, and it caught in his throat as his body froze. Clint took advantage of his stillness to rain several more slaps of fire on his ass, and it was then Jace began to struggle. His cock was dripping and his hips rocked, looking for relief, but the part of his brain that was trying to keep it all under wraps knew it would all come out with the release. And so he fought it with everything he had, but it was no use—Clint was too good. Too strong.

Jace wasn't sure if he hated or loved the man and figured the truth was probably a little bit of both.

Every time he moved, the urge to come got stronger, but he knew what the fallout would be. He bucked, and somehow it only cemented Clint's position of strength over him.

He would need to surrender, and it should be easy to put everything into the man's more-than-competent hands. But nothing in his life had been, and maybe he didn't believe it should start now.

Everything swirled inside his mind, and then, without warning, it came to a head as Clint delivered a series of quick, intense slaps, stopped and told him, "I think you need daily spankings to keep you level, and I'll bend you over my knee every single time I see you." At those words, Jace exploded, climaxed with the force of multiple orgasms—a first—as his body tensed with complete and utter pleasure.

The second release immediately followed, a gut-wrenching sob that stole his breath as he finally gave in.

Jace's surrender broke Clint's heart and made him happy at the same time. He righted the boy, undid his cuffs and held him in his lap, their come still on their stomachs and chests, both sweating, and Jace probably didn't realize Clint had shed a few tears of his own during the ordeal.

But this was about Jace and the loss of his teammates, the overpowering feeling of helplessness, and Clint knew it all too well.

"I would take it all away if I could," Clint told him.

"I'd take you up on that," Jace mumbled. His eyes were heavy-lidded, but most importantly, his body and mind had finally relaxed. "Why?"

"Why what?'

"Why do I need this?"

Clint stroked a hand across his cheek. "Because you like it. Because it helps. Who the hell cares about why? There's nothing wrong with needing it at all. Nothing. I never want you to feel bad about wanting things rough. Or sweet. Or upside-fucking-down."

Jace's response was a small smile and the press of a kiss to the front of Clint's neck, right into the dip where his neck met collarbone. And just that small touch was enough to get Clint hard.

Jace knew it, because he kissed his way down Clint's chest as Clint rolled to his back and let Jace give him a blowjob that made his head nearly blow off.

An hour later, Jace had allowed Clint to clean them both up and order dinner, and they tucked into the couch with cartons of Chinese food as Jace alternately ate and slept.

Finally, around five p.m., he was alert, polished off whatever food was left and looked for more.

Yes, he was better. Just in time for Clint to leave.

"What time do you go?" Jace asked, startling him.

"Mind reader?"

"You've got that look."

Clint knew it—he'd been detaching already, even with Jace in his arms, and he stopped that and brought himself back to the present and the next hours he did have with Jace.

The next job was in Yemen, a mission that promised at least two months of deep, underground undercover with an intricate set of plans that could easily get him killed. He'd already memorized them, gone over fifty different options for E & E, and he still felt like he hadn't planned enough.

When he came out of his CIA-induced reverie, Jace was watching him with a small smile.

"Sorry."

"You've got to do what keeps you safe. That's all I want."

"Really? The only thing?" he teased as he rubbed Jace's ass, and Jace blushed and winced at the same time. "Come here, baby, I've got plenty of time for more."

Jace didn't hesitate, climbed into his lap and kissed him, tasting like lo mein and beer and man, and Clint knew he'd remember that taste forever. Wanted to.

But first, Clint needed Jace to talk about what he was dealing with. And so he pulled back and he waited, and finally Jace mock-sighed and relented.

"I'm sure you know what happened," he muttered, and it was true. Clint had spoken to Rex earlier.

"I know you saved a lot of people on this trip, despite how it ended."

"You're not going to give me the survivor's guilt, are you?"

"Do I need to?" Jace shook his head, and Clint pulled him close and continued, "On top of whatever else you're feeling, you should be feeling grateful."

"For what?"

"That you can still feel. You care. The second you lose that, you've lost everything."

Jace propped himself up. "That's not you."

"I've always defined myself by my job. It's what I'm built for, Jace. What I'm good at."

"You're more than that."

"For you, I want to be. If you hadn't rescued me that night..." he started. "Dammit, Jace, you really rescued me. And I'm not talking about from bullets. If I'd done that job, I didn't know if I'd have been able to extricate myself. I was getting pulled under...you stopped me from losing myself. You made me feel, and I almost hated you for it."

"You have a funny way of showing hate," Jace said, his voice hoarse.

"You slayed me."

"I can't be sorry for that."

"I don't want you to be. I don't think I'll ever be good enough for you, but for the first time in my life, I love enough to want to try. You pulled me back off the ledge. And that's why I'll track you down every time. You're too important to lose."

Jace didn't know what to say to that, and there wasn't anything to say. Instead, he wrapped his arms around the bigger man and held him for a change. Clint pushed his cheek against Jace's shoulder, sinking into the embrace without protest.

Maybe it was time for Jace to stop protesting about everything. Giving in to Clint was so much easier, and for sure, satisfying.

The one thing standing in the way nagged at Jace, and he couldn't push it down. But he didn't let go of Clint. "It's too much sometimes. I don't know if I can do it, Clint. I don't know—but then I do it and it's okay. But it's like climbing a fucking mountain every single morning of my life."

"I know, baby boy. I really do." Clint massaged the back of Jace's neck, and Jace groaned his appreciation.

"It doesn't get easier."

"Never."

"Shit," Jace muttered, bent his head forward, and they remained like that for a while, until Clint made him lie facedown on the bed and massaged his back, put cream on his aching ass. And still his mind wasn't calmed completely, but he knew that he'd be able to sleep again, at least.

"I guess I need to thank you."

"You just need to call me—that's all," Clint told him. "You have to let me in."

"I'm doing that, Clint. You don't fucking realize—"

"I do." He ran his hands through Jace's hair to get it off his face and then broached the subject they'd left off on four months earlier. "Listen, please, you've got enough shit with your job. You don't need this club—"

"I have to help Kenny," Jace said wearily, the admission sliding out before he could help it. "I mean, I can't let him be alone."

"He's in it hardcore. You know you can't get him out,

163

Jace—you know that."

Jace almost told him then, about the deal he'd made with the Feds and that he was afraid he was getting screwed, but everything was so entwined.

And then Clint said, "There's been a tail on several members who've met with the Colombians through the new warehouse."

Kenny was one of them. That was Clint's unspoken message, something that Jace knew already.

He wished Clint hadn't shared that, although he was grateful for Kenny's sake.

"You need to get out—Kenny's made his bed."

"If I'm around, they won't touch him."

Clint didn't argue. Jace knew his own statement was more true than false, but that didn't mean Jace was safe by any means. But Clint continued, "If you want, I can—"

"No." If the Feds knew Jace had involved another agency, that would be worse.

"I know that once you're in the MC, there are only a few options for getting out, all of them either painful or undesirable," Clint said now, and Jace nodded, although they both knew they'd resolved nothing more on the subject.

Torn between love and family, he was in the shittiest place possible, and since Clint was out and safe, Jace figured he could only hope for the best.

Chapter Twenty-Two

After the long-assed mission followed up by the head-splitting tragedy, Sawyer went home with a heavy heart and brooded. And drank. And brooded and drank and called Jace, who didn't answer. Which meant his friend couldn't stop him from doing the stupidest thing ever, which was why he found himself at Rex's door with the bottle of Jack still in his hands and the cab that drove him here long gone.

He prepped for a long, humiliating walk home in the pouring rain and took another drink for courage. And stumbled back and cursed when the bottle broke and the lights went on inside the house, and he thought about running. But then the door opened and Rex stood there in just shorts, looking sleepy and so damned good.

It was too late to back down now. He stood and braced himself for Rex to yell, but all the man did was open the door while Sawyer continued to stand in the soaking rain.

Finally, he managed, "I...had a nightmare." Could he *be* any lamer?

"And you decided coming here drunk to share that intel was a good idea?" Rex asked, and although Sawyer couldn't be one hundred percent certain, he was pretty sure that Rex's tone was...almost teasing. And he had that little twisted smile on his face, the one Sawyer sometimes caught him using when he looked at him when he thought Sawyer wasn't watching.

"You didn't call tonight. You've been calling, and—" His stomach fluttered, and he kept going. "I know I piss you off all the time when we're not on the phone."

"You don't."

"Then why the fuck are you always yelling at me?" It came out in an exasperated tumble and probably more demanding that he should be with his CO, regardless of the fact that his visit was anything but professional. And he crossed his arms and waited for Rex's reply, which he wasn't prepared for.

"I push you because I need you to train as hard as you can so nothing ever happens to you," Rex said quietly, his eyes shining with an emotion Sawyer couldn't place. But there was something dark there. The man was in mourning himself, just like the rest of them.

Had it always really been that simple of an explanation? Sawyer swallowed back what would've been a laugh and a sob all at once, and at the same time he moved forward.

Rex waited, let Sawyer embrace him and kiss him without any hesitation. The time for hesitating was long gone, and when his mouth met Rex's, the fear he'd been holding on to stripped away for the moment. His hands sought quarter on Rex's shoulders, his wet clothes hit Rex's bare chest with a satisfying slap and his tongue dueled with his CO's in a dance older than time.

He met no resistance—Rex kissed him back immediately, wrapped his arms around Sawyer's waist and dragged him first closer and then into the living room, where they tumbled to the couch, breaking the kiss only when Rex pulled Sawyer's shirt off. Somehow, Sawyer was in his lap, straddling him, and they were both soaking wet and so was the couch.

And then Sawyer rested his forehead against Rex's for a

long moment, the only sounds their harsh breathing as he tried to reconcile what had just happened and what was to come.

"You okay?" Rex asked finally.

He couldn't look Rex in the eye yet. Kept them closed, forehead to forehead. "More than. It's just that...I've never..."

"I figured."

"Should I be insulted?"

Rex laughed softly. "If it wasn't your first time, you wouldn't have made me wait this long."

Sawyer went to pull away, embarrassed, but Rex pulled him back. "It was sweet, watching you wrestle with your feelings."

"Sweet? Christ," Sawyer mumbled. "Was I that obvious?"

"Only to me. But you were worth the wait." Rex traced the path of Sawyer's jaw with his finger. "You have no idea how tough it was not to pull you in the shower with me. Or not to follow you into your bunk afterward and go down on you."

Sawyer drew a stuttered breath and his cock jumped.

"You would've let me, right?"

"I think I might've," Sawyer whispered. "You're so strong, Rex. So big and strong, and you make me feel safe."

"You do the same to me."

Sawyer's eyes met Rex's and there was no joke in them. "Thanks for saying that."

Rex stroked a hand through his hair, then pulled him in for a kiss. Sawyer ground against him like he was unable to control his body.

Like he didn't want to. "The phone calls helped."

But Rex pulled back. "You have to be ready."

"I am." Sawyer put Rex's hand on his swollen cock. "Now

fuck me."

"Now you're giving me the orders?" Rex asked, his eyebrow raised, his voice shooting straight to Sawyer's cock.

"Yes," he answered boldly.

"I don't want to do this when you're too drunk to make a decision."

"I'm not." It was the truth—Rex's admission and the kiss had sobered him in a way he hadn't thought possible. Although the buzz was flowing through his body, he figured the liquid courage would help to hide his nervousness of being a freakin' virgin again. "Please...don't make me wait. I've already done that for too long. I don't want to waste any more time."

"Talking to you, being with you, isn't something I'd ever consider to be wasted time," Rex told him. "You didn't really have a nightmare."

"Couldn't even get to sleep," he admitted.

"Pretty normal after the kind of tragedy we faced today."

"Nothing feels normal," Sawyer said. "But some things, they just feel right."

Rex swallowed hard. Sawyer watched the man's Adam's apple move, the only movement on the man's body. When Rex wanted to be, he was an immovable brick wall—and Sawyer wanted nothing more than for the wall to break, just a little.

He's probably wanting the same thing from you.

Tonight, they'd both get what they wanted.

The boy was drunk as shit—and although Rex didn't doubt for a second Sawyer was there of his own free will, his conscience couldn't let him do what his cock so desperately wanted. He knew Sawyer wouldn't take no for an answer, so he dragged the boy's jeans off and put him in bed, letting the hard planes of the boy's body jut into his.

He'd underestimated how strong his SEAL was, when the boy jerked his own shorts off and circled Rex's cock, his breath catching when he did so. Rex stilled, willing himself not to come in Sawyer's hand.

"Sawyer, please...I want you sober when we do this the first time."

But Sawyer was beyond listening, was stroking and teasing, and it had been too long coming. Rex let out a strangled groan as the drunken boy took control of him, pushing him back, taking his cock in his mouth, and for someone who had no experience...

"Sawyer, Christ..." Rex bucked his hips up as Sawyer suckled him hard, just the way he liked it.

He hadn't expected the tables to turn like this, but luckily for Sawyer, he was willing to be patient. Which honestly wasn't very patient at all, although the way Sawyer was fucking his cock with his mouth was helping a lot.

He wanted to pull out, turn the boy over and fuck him, wanted to tell himself that they had nothing but time tonight and tomorrow, but he knew that wasn't true. All they had was what they had at that moment, and to not take the risk would result in regrets. And Rex had too many of those.

"Sawyer, I'm going to come in your mouth if you don't move away now," he warned, which only resulted in Sawyer taking him in more deeply. He felt him gag a little, but Rex shot anyway, and Sawyer held his hips tightly, like he was afraid the prize would be taken from him because he wasn't perfect.

But he was so fucking perfect, Rex couldn't stand it. And when he could finally move again, he dragged Sawyer to him, tasted himself in the boy's mouth as their kiss melded them together. Rain poured down around the house, drumming the roof, slamming the windows, and that rhythm was inherent in Rex's brain. He wanted to pound into Sawyer to the same beat.

He reached out a hand to grab the lube in his drawer. Squeezed some on his fingers and began to work them down inside Sawyer's ass as the boy stiffened. He watched Sawyer's face carefully, memorizing those first expressions as his fingers stroked and circled and finally entered, slowly at first and then more insistently as Sawyer moaned with pure pleasure.

Sawyer, up on his hands and knees, looking down as Rex finger-fucked him, and Rex would never, ever forget this moment, like it was frozen in time.

"More, Rex. I want more."

"Good, because you're going to get it." Two fingers now, and he maneuvered so Sawyer was on his back, legs spread, surrendering to the inevitable.

"I loved watching you in the shower," Sawyer confessed with a gasp. "But this is better."

"Yeah," Rex agreed, adding a third finger, opening the boy up for him. Sawyer was watching him, and the sensations rolling through his body made him relaxed enough to take it.

Whether he'd regret it in the morning was still a nagging thought in the back of Rex's mind. And, as if Sawyer knew, he reached up and touched the man's jaw.

"I want this. Wanted it forever," he told Rex fiercely. "Want to be fucked by you and held by you."

"In the morning you might get nervous."

"Suppose I do? Suppose I bolt?"

"I'll bring you back, because this is where you belong," Rex told him as he twisted his fingers, and Sawyer's hips rose up as he howled.

As hard as his dick was, he wanted Sawyer far more lucid

before they fucked for the first time. Wanted his eyes and his mind clear. And so he brushed the boy's prostate again and again, used his free hand to stroke Sawyer's cock, watched as the spiraled loss of control overtook him.

"Yeah, that's nice, boy—you look so hot when you're on the brink like this," Rex told him, because Sawyer was helpless and enjoying it, and finally, the boy closed his eyes and came so hard he spurted his chest and chin and some of the headboard behind him.

"Beautiful," Rex murmured against him, his hand still half inside Sawyer's ass, his tongue licking the side of the boy's neck, tasting sweat and man.

Sawyer looked content as a whole, but something in his eyes told Rex he still held on to some worry. "What are you afraid of?" Rex asked him.

"That this isn't real. That you'll realize I'm not good enough for you."

"It's real, and you're more than good enough, Sawyer. And I'll tell you what—if you bolt, I'll come after you."

"You're sure?"

"I don't give my word lightly. You run, I follow—at least in the beginning. Once you're on solid footing, I don't expect you to be scared anymore."

The adrenaline rush and the alcohol, combined with the orgasm and the stress of the day, took over, as Rex hoped. Soon, Sawyer was drooling on his shoulder, and Rex pulled the covers around them and hoped that morning didn't bring on another attack of Sawyer's nerves.

The boy was safe though, and that was all that mattered to Rex that night. Mourning their lost comrades was something they'd do every time they did their jobs. But tonight was for acceptance. Sawyer had finally come to him.

Clint called Styx. Good thing the man was good with late-night, cryptic, out-of-the-blue phone calls, because this would definitely be one of them.

"To be a good agent, you don't share anything, which makes you shit in a relationship," he started.

To his credit, Styx answered Clint's couched question immediately, his voice obviously rough from sleep. "But you're with a guy who gets your world."

"It's still dangerous to let him in. For him, for me."

"He's not a civilian—he can take care of himself," Styx told him. "And yes, I realize it took me sixteen years to realize that about Law. But I don't want to see someone I care about waste a minute. Wasted time brings nothing but regrets."

Styx was right. Everything was a risk, but diving in deep with Jace was a good risk to take.

"There are people who want to hurt me by taking anyone who's important to me."

"I know—that's the most effective way to take a spook down." Special forces operators lived by a similar code, much less secreted than Delta, and pictures of SEALs were never published, let alone names.

"I've never had to worry about that."

"I guess it depends on what you want. If you're happy with the way things were when you weren't attached."

"I wouldn't be happy letting go of Jace," Clint admitted.

"Then don't."

Chapter Twenty-Three

Jace had shitty dreams throughout the night, but Clint had woken him each and every time. Held him. Talked him down.

"Suppose you weren't here?"

"But I am. Always will be, in one form or another."

For the first time since Clint had proposed it, Jace was taking Clint's offer of retirement very seriously. Very seriously. But there was still the whole business with Kenny and the threats the Feds made to him.

He'd begun to suspect that his handler asked him the questions about Tomcat because they suspected a relationship of some kind, either before Tomcat's "death" or afterward when they'd realized he was an agent.

A lot of speculation for sure, but what if the Feds ever got wind of the fact that Jace was with a CIA agent? When he felt trapped with no way out, bad shit happened.

Don't go there, he warned himself. He already had one set of scars from before he went into the Navy—these new ones just added another layer.

He ran his hands through his hair and thought about joining Clint in the shower when his phone rang. It was a number he didn't recognize, but he picked it up because it might've been an MC person, or it could just be some asshole who had a wrong number.

"Hey Jace, it's Jack. I'm Clint's friend."

As he listened, he realized it was some asshole, but he didn't have the wrong number at all.

When Clint got out of the shower, Jace was lying on the bed, staring at the ceiling. He glanced over and asked, "Who's Jack?"

Well, hello, left field. "He's just someone I've known for a long time."

"You slept with him."

"Yes."

Jace nodded, as if somehow pleased with Clint's easy admission. "He called for you."

"You answered my phone?" Clint asked.

Jace glared at him. "He called mine."

Shit. He was dialing Jack back without waiting to hear more from Jace, who rolled off the bed and headed downstairs. Jace didn't seem particularly upset, but he'd have to talk to the boy about it. But first, he needed to deal with a former fuck-buddy gone rogue.

"Hey, Clint—figured I'd hear from you." Jack's voice was a deep, easy drawl. "I'm in town, so I figured..."

"We've had this discussion," Clint said tightly.

"Come on—you expect me to take that shit seriously?"

"Take it seriously, Jack. And if you ever call Jace again—"

But Jack had already hung up, and Clint doubted he'd heard the last of the guy. He should've been ready for that but never figured that Jack's feelings ran any deeper than Clint's own, which had been more of the quick, safe fuck variety than anything deeper.

He still owed Jace an explanation, even though the boy hadn't asked for one. He went back into the bedroom and pulled on a pair of jeans before heading downstairs barefoot, finding Jace rooting through the fridge.

The bruises on his back from the recent mission were looking worse than they had last night, and Clint couldn't resist reaching out to rub them lightly. Jace looked over his shoulder.

"I'll make you some breakfast," he offered, and Jace shrugged, moved out of the way to let Clint grab the eggs and bacon and bread. As he got everything together, he said, "I never gave him your number."

"Then how did he get it? How would he know we're together?" Jace demanded, and yeah, there was the anger.

"He was helping on the MC op," Clint explained. "We had everyone's number. What are you more pissed about—the fact that I slept with him or that he knows about your personal life?" Clint wasn't sure which he was hoping for.

Jace paused for a long moment before saying, "He knows we're involved. He told me that I was just a fuck to you, that you'd never taken it seriously. That you were using me until he got back into town. That you'd been fucking for the past seven years and that you always came back to him."

Jace waited for Clint to refute any of it. He wanted to, but for some reason, all that came out was, "We all have complications."

"How complicated are yours?" Jace asked.

"Look, we weren't exactly exclusive after a weekend together."

"So we won't be," Jace shot back, and that made Clint see

red.

God, the boy was purposely being such an asshole. After everything that happened last night, you'd think he'd learn to let his guard down. "I don't want to picture you with anyone else."

Jace gave a one-shoulder shrug. "I'm not a genie, and I don't grant wishes."

Clint threw down the bread he'd been playing with opening and went to Jace, pulled him up from the chair and into his arms. "I don't want to be with anyone else. I told him that months ago—he's just having trouble getting the message."

As he looked into Jace's eyes, he thought back to the night Tomcat officially died. Remembered watching the explosion that ended up killing another MC member, although that hadn't been part of the plan. That the collateral damage had been a murdering thug had been of some comfort, but Clint had never been into playing God.

"You did good, Clint," his handler told him, and it was the first time he'd heard his real name spoken out loud in years. And he hadn't felt like Clint at all, just felt empty.

"I'd been thinking about you a lot," he told Jace now. "I was planning on cutting you off before it got too hard. And then..."

Jack had been waiting for him at the safe house two weeks after Clint had retired Tomcat, two weeks after the explosion, when he'd realized he couldn't sleep with Jack anymore.

"Hey, you avoiding me?" Jack had asked, and there was no use denying it any longer. He hadn't seen Jace visiting his grave at the cemetery yet, but he'd known he would see Jace again.

"There's someone else," he'd said before he could stop himself. He wasn't supposed to see Jace at all after the job was done, but Jace knew about his cover. So he justified that technically, he could see the boy again.

176

So when are you going to tell Jace?

He'd waited until Jace got home to do so, even then wasn't sure. But when he saw pictures of Jace at his grave...well, that had nearly killed him.

"So after the bomb went off, you fucked someone else to make yourself feel better?" Jace asked.

Clint could do nothing but nod and say, "I don't expect you to understand."

"Good."

"I was numb, for Christ's sake."

"Obviously not that numb," Jace muttered. "Fucking was the last thing on my mind."

"We all handle grief differently," Clint said, and that's when Jace punched him, a left hook that caught his cheek and took him to the ground.

"Don't pull your bullshit platitudes with me. You wanted to fuck and so you did. You didn't owe me anything, other than honesty."

Clint rubbed his cheek and tried to keep his temper in check. "You don't want to fight me, boy."

"Yeah, I do. I want to fight with you until I feel better, but I'm not sure you could take it." Jace's eyes blazed as he spoke.

"I guess we handle things differently."

"Why can't you say how you feel without spitting out what you think you're supposed to?"

"I fucked Jack, and I pretended it was you—is that what you want to hear?"

"It's a start," Jace ground out. "Was I any good?"

"You're a real son of a bitch, you know that?"

"You're just figuring that out? Look, I get it. Now he wants

177

you because he can't have you," Jace assessed, but the anger was gone from his voice.

"I've known him for a long time. I guess I misread the situation. But I don't think I'm misreading this one, baby. I've been thinking about how I'd feel if you came to me and told me there was someone else. For a while, I didn't think I could blame you, because I knew I couldn't give you every day."

"I couldn't give you that either. I never asked for that—you offered."

"I know I did. If that's what you want, I'll find a way. I've been waiting for you to tell me what you want."

Jace just blinked hard. "You don't have to say that to prove you're sorry about Jack."

"That's not why I'm saying it. I wasn't saying it in the hotel because you were hurt and pissed, either. You know that."

"Yeah, I do." Jace reached up to put a hand behind Clint's neck. "There's been no one since you that night in your apartment. No one. And trust me, this isn't exactly a convenience."

Clint laughed softly as Jace pulled him closer for a kiss.

When they broke apart, Jace said, "You really think we can make this work beyond what we have?"

"I think we'd both do well in jobs we had more control over."

"That can't all be for me."

"It's not—and I don't mean that in a bad way. But I'm content with what I've done. If you weren't in the picture, I probably wouldn't have considered this. But you are." Clint watched him. "Am I alone on this goddamned ledge?"

"No." Jace's word was a whisper, the emotion choking him, and Clint took it as a good sign, especially when he added, "I'd explore the being-with-you-more-often thing, if there was really a way."

Clint nodded, and for the first time, he realized he could seriously consider without freaking the thought of leaving the CIA behind. "I'll find one. But for now, you know there's no one else for me. Won't be."

"I'm not really that hungry right this second. Not for breakfast, anyway," Jace told him, but Clint was already putting him at the table.

Were a series of relationship encounters enough to solidify their relationship for the rest of their lives? So far, Clint thought so.

"We have a lot more than most couples who are together daily have," Clint reminded Jace, because it was the truth. Their time together might be brief, but they made the most of it. And they understood each other—the jobs, the secrecy. The fact that sometimes they were so wired after a mission that they couldn't handle noise or touches or even company well all meant that they had a good handle on each other.

"We do have a lot of sex in this relationship."

"The best ones do," Clint pointed out. "If you don't think that every time I fuck you, I'm telling you something, you're wrong."

"Are you doing this because you want me—or because you want to make sure no one else will have me?" Jace demanded.

"I don't want anyone else to have you, but I want you. That's the truth." Clint eyed him. "Is there someone else?"

"No."

"I never want there to be. All right?"

Jace nodded, bit his bottom lip. "Yeah, it's more than all right."

SE Jakes

Sawyer opened his eyes and blinked at the too-bright sunlight. It took him several moments before he could actually move, and when he did, his head pounded.

Once he realized he wasn't actually in his own place, the events of last night came pouring back over him. He reached for the tags on the bed next to him, and reading them confirmed everything.

They were Rex's. And he probably had made a complete fool of himself coming here. Or had he? It was so damned fuzzy, and when he sat up, he realized how sore his ass was. And how alone he was.

He dressed quickly, made it down the beach and to his apartment in twenty minutes. He was still shaking after an equally long, hot shower, tried to blame it on the alcohol, although he knew it had nothing to do with it.

They hadn't done much, but Sawyer knew he'd been pretty insistent. He remembered Rex told him that he wanted to wait until Sawyer was sober—Sawyer still didn't think he was, despite the ten hours that had passed. And Sawyer wasn't sure what he was upset at, because he'd been dreaming about waking up in Rex's bed for months.

And then you ran. Idiot. He put his head in his hands, looked up only when he heard his front door open. In seconds, Rex was in front of him.

"Get dressed. Pack a bag," Rex said, and there was no arguing with him. Rex watched him the entire time as Sawyer's cheeks burned. Finally, he followed Rex out the door and into the car.

As the truck rolled back toward Rex's house, Rex pointed to the hot coffee.

180

"Thanks."

"You ran off pretty fast."

"I was...really busy."

Rex laughed at that, long, loud and without a trace of malice. His hand landed on Sawyer's thigh, and Sawyer's cock rose at the touch.

Rex wasn't angry. He was...he understood. Sawyer relaxed a little as Rex drove the truck into his garage. As the door closed behind them, Rex said, "Remember what I told you last night, when you said you were scared?"

It took several moments for Sawyer to reel back to that place from last night, when his brain had fogged from whiskey and lust.

"'You'll try to bolt, and I'll come after you as long as I think you really want to come back'."

He spoke out loud, jerked to look at Rex, who was waiting by the open passenger's side door. He nodded, pulled Sawyer's bag over his shoulder.

"Let's go have some breakfast."

Sawyer followed him inside, sat at the table while Rex cooked for him, his mind still spinning that the big man doing so was the same one who screamed at him on a regular basis.

"I didn't mean to make you go out of your way," he started.

"I know," Rex said simply, put a plate of eggs, bacon and toast in front of him, and Sawyer realized he was starving. He dug into the food and Rex ate, too, and the talk was easy.

They watched TV, rested. A couple of hours later, Rex wound himself around Sawyer—by that time, all he wanted was the bigger man's body to cover his, to be fucked and fucked good.

Rex took his sweet time, as Sawyer groaned in frustration.

Rex chuckled softly before his mouth covered Sawyer's cock.

Sawyer bucked, and then Rex held his hips down—his eyes never leaving Sawyer's face, which was probably what made it hotter, because Sawyer couldn't look away. Couldn't hide anything, couldn't tear his gaze away.

All he could do was revel in the complete pleasure Rex was giving him.

His legs spread wantonly over Rex's shoulders, Rex telling him to just sit back and enjoy. But he had to touch Rex just to make sure all of this wasn't a dream.

Sawyer ran his hands over Rex's smooth, shaved head—and the whole time, Rex watched and sucked on him until Sawyer's toes curled, most of the nervousness subsided and he came.

"Rex, I'm...fuck..." Rex knew, sucked harder, his fingers playing along Sawyer's exposed hole, and as he shot, Rex put a finger inside of him, which caused the orgasm to last for fucking ever.

Sawyer was sweating and was pretty sure he yelled loud enough to wake the neighbors.

Rex seemed nonchalant. For all Sawyer knew, there was a steady stream of yelling, well-blown guys through this place. But he didn't really believe that. Not the way Rex looked at him. Not the way he'd come to get him.

Chapter Twenty-Four

Jace had been at the hospital all night after he'd gotten Kenny's call. Clint was there waiting for him when he got home, which Jace was grateful for. Clint's missions came up fast, and Jace leaving him in the house in the morning wasn't any reassurance that he'd come home to him.

Then again, Clint didn't have that with Jace, either. But Jace was beginning to want it the other way. Clint's words had given him a hope he hadn't had before this.

"Rough night?"

"Shit with Kenny." Clint shot him a warning look, but Jace waved it off. "I had to bail him out."

"What did he do?"

"Cage fighting. Again."

"Dammit."

"I just left him in the hospital. They're hoping they don't have to remove his spleen. He has no goddamned insurance." Jace sank to the couch and ran his hands through his hair. "I can't deal with this shit for much longer."

The first time, Kenny had miraculously won—Jace knew they probably put him up against someone easy to keep him lured in. But now, with the MC betting on him—or against him, if necessary—the fights would only get tougher. Kenny was big, yes, but he wasn't a fight-until-you-die type.

And Jace had a feeling he was going to have to become one to survive this. "Didn't mean to ditch you tonight."

"It's all right. I spent the evening catching up with Styx and his partners."

"Partners as in...CIA?"

"Partners as in relationship."

"That sounds way more fun to talk about than dealing with Kenny. So they're together—all three of them?" Jace asked. "How exactly does that work?"

"Apparently, really well. Why, you looking to add a third?" Clint demanded.

"Dude, I can barely handle you."

"Don't flatter me, boy—or I'll—"

"Put me over your knee?" Jace asked slyly.

"I've created a monster, haven't I?" Clint asked. "Seriously, I'd like you to meet them."

Jace nodded. "I'd like that."

Big steps for them, Jace supposed. And it felt good.

It was hours later when Clint dressed for his next mission and Jace waited and watched from the bed. It was 0300 and neither had slept, because sleep didn't seem nearly as important as just being together.

Yeah, Clint could do with this peaceful feeling all the damned time. Wondered how long it would remain once he left Jace, and got his answer before he even exited the boy's house. His phone rang, and it was his handler and supervisor, Pete.

He dealt with the MC stuff still, kept his hand in because of Jace, mainly, although to his supervisor, it looked like he simply cared about a mission he'd put everything he had into.

"Are they ever going to move on the intel I gave them?" Clint asked Pete.

"Over the next two weeks. They're using the plants you provided to breathe things down among the ranks."

So there would be a bust in the MC gang soon. Clint figured it was a matter of time before the whole thing folded like a house of cards, and he knew how worried Jace was about his cousin.

Telling Jace violated everything, but there was no way around it. And hell, if it meant keeping Jace safe, he didn't give a damn.

"You still there, Clint?"

"Yeah, sorry."

"The DEA wants you to run a workshop for its newly promoted undercover agents," Pete told him. "I signed you up."

Clint wanted to argue because he hated teaching. Sitting and talking was never anything like the real mission. Instead, he asked, "Keep me updated on the bust, all right?"

"You're never this interested in your cases once you're done," Pete pointed out.

"Never did one that encompassed years of my life. I'd like to see some satisfaction," Clint told him, and hell, that was the truth, for sure.

Clint's demeanor had changed after he'd gotten the call. Jace figured it had something to do with the MC and cursed inwardly.

SE Jakes

He hadn't been able to find out more intel from Kenny about the gun-running operations he was on the periphery of, because his cousin was too scared to tell him much. And Jace hadn't exactly had tons of time to hang around the MC, so his intel gathering was at a standstill. He'd hoped to put in some time there over the next few days before he reported back to base.

"Hey." Clint picked up his bag. "Don't go near the club for the next few weeks."

"Why?"

"Just fucking promise me, okay?" Clint growled, and Jace's stomach dropped. Clint was warning him that the CIA was ready to move in and make a huge bust, and Kenny—fuck, Kenny would be taken away if Jace didn't alert the Feds.

He couldn't betray Clint like that—the man had worked too hard, and Jace would fuck up everything, including Clint's career and anything the men had between them. "Okay, yeah, I'll stay away."

"You know what I'm risking, telling you this, right?"

"I'd never fucking betray you."

"I know. It's the only reason I'm sharing this intel." Clint sighed. "Kenny's going to be involved—there's no way around it."

Jace knew—taking Kenny away now would look suspicious and could only happen if the Feds hid him. The MC would think Kenny was a rat, and they'd search for him, but he'd be well hidden. "I won't say anything."

Clint just gave him a hard, one-armed hug, the other still holding his heavy bag of tricks. Jace buried his face in the man's jacket, inhaling his scent as if it would let him track Clint across the globe.

186

If only it were that easy.

Clint tried again as he pulled away. "Please reconsider getting out."

"I want to, but I can't leave Kenny alone in there. I know he was stupid to get involved. But I understand why he did it. He said that, for the first time, he felt important. Part of something bigger. He had power. Back-up. Kenny was pretty scrawny growing up. I kind of watched over him, fought some of his battles. Maybe I should've let him deal with more of it on his own."

"Jace, this isn't your fault."

Jace didn't believe that for a second. "Look, all I know is that I can't leave him alone. He's in real danger. He's scared shitless, and they're dragging him in deeper and deeper because they smell his fear. They're worried he'll talk—and they'll kill him if they so much as suspect he's thinking of leaving."

"They're getting him into the drug trade," Clint muttered.

"And if your bust happens soon...well, he's screwed. I have a small window to get him out."

"What are you going to do—fake his death?" Clint asked. "Everything you're doing is putting your career—and more importantly, your life—in jeopardy."

"I'll be careful, Clint."

Finally, Clint nodded and kissed him fiercely, and then he left, walking down the path without looking back, because it was, Jace understood, the only way to make the break.

Jace did the same, closing the door so he couldn't hear the car pull away, and he sat at the table with clenched fists for a long while before making any kind of move. Finally, an hour later, he picked up the phone and called Mike.

"Jace, what's going on?"

SE Jakes

"I don't think I can do this anymore."

"You don't have a choice."

"I can take care of Kenny on my own," Jace said firmly.

"What do you think your CO will say when I tell him about all of this?"

"Don't you dare fucking threaten me. I've given you enough information that could've gotten me killed, and you haven't moved on it. It's been a year—I didn't agree to a lifetime of indentured servitude, and it's not my fault you can't get one of your own in there successfully," Jace told him, managing to keep his voice even and unthreatening even though he was anything but calm, cool and collected. There was time to break down and blow up later.

"Jace, you can't get out now. That's all I'm telling you. Maybe in another couple of months, depending on what you give us—"

Jace cut the line and dialed Kenny at the hospital. "How's it going?"

"I'm all right. Spleen's getting better. Gotta stay in here for another day and then go home to rest. Gotta get better for next week. Cools said there's something big happening, and he invited me to be a part of it."

Fuck, of course he did. "Kenny—"

"I can't say no, man. You said to keep it even and not let them know I'm scared shitless. This was one of those you-can't-refuse-it kinds of offers, so I didn't."

Kenny sounded short of breath, and Jace ran his hands through his hair and thanked his lucky stars that none of it was happening immediately. And hell, even if it was, he couldn't force Kenny not to do something—and that was becoming more and more apparent. "No, it's all right. I understand. Just take

188

care of yourself and call me if you need a ride from the hospital when they release you. We'll deal with next week when it happens."

He hung up the phone and buried his face in his hands.

Chapter Twenty-Five

For Sawyer, the next days and weeks were a balancing act. On base, Rex acted the way he always did, and Sawyer tried to do the same. Had to, or else he'd have to leave the teams before he endangered anyone.

At night, though, that was a different story. Rex would come get him and bring him back to his place, but Rex wouldn't let him stay over—drove him home at night after they'd been together. Said it was so no one caught them, but Sawyer had a feeling something deeper was going on, and he was determined not to be dissuaded.

Tonight, he was going to find out what that was. It was the first time he'd really been able to explore Rex's body—without the haze of alcohol or interruption or his newness getting in the way—and he wouldn't be persuaded to stop.

Rex was asleep—or maybe pretending to be—when Sawyer climbed into bed next to him and drew back the sheets a bit. Went to massage his shoulders, and Rex stiffened under the touch.

"I should get you back home," Rex said sleepily. "Didn't mean to—"

"What? Rest?" Sawyer moved his hands over Rex's shoulders, and the man didn't protest this time. Not yet, anyway. "Besides, I'm staying tonight."

"Sawyer—"

"What? I'm not invited?"

Rex put his head back down on the pillow and didn't say anything for a long while, just let Sawyer massage the kinks out of his neck and shoulders from the day's training.

Finally, without looking at him, Rex said, "We've got a busy day of training tomorrow."

Sawyer got off him and rooted around for his clothes. "Got it, loud and clear."

"Sawyer, look—"

"Forget it." Sawyer tried to brush it off like it was nothing and failed miserably.

But Rex was up, grabbing him by the shoulders. "You're not ready."

"For what?"

"For all of this. You're ready to bail at any second still—I can see it—and I'm not ready to give everything to someone who's not all there."

"Maybe you'll never be ready, because I'll always be second."

"That's not true."

"Bullshit it's not." Sawyer yanked himself away and went down the stairs, finished pulling his jeans on. He walked out and was halfway to his car before he realized that Rex wasn't going to follow him. Halfway home before he realized just how badly that hurt.

The fallout Clint had mentioned didn't happen until two weeks after Clint left. The aftermath continued long after that, however, so much so that when Jace returned from a two-week mission, he found messages from Cools requesting him to come into the club immediately, that he needed to talk to Jace about possibly getting out of the club for his own safety.

He couldn't deny Cools was right about that, but he highly doubted the MC's president had Jace's best interests at heart.

He hadn't even had a chance to talk to Kenny—the guy wasn't answering his phone and the texts had all been terse, and Jace gave up and figured they were monitoring Kenny's phone.

He'd posted bail for Kenny through the bondsman when he'd been on his way to Afghanistan and got the text his cousin had been released about four hours later. Couldn't let his cousin sit in jail indefinitely—there were too many other gang members on the inside, and that could be a far more vicious environment.

It was a smaller bust than Jace thought, or maybe it was just the CIA's way of feeling things out.

"You got him out fast," Cools said now.

Jace explained that Kenny couldn't miss another night's work or he'd be fired. The club still had him gun-running and cage fighting, but Jace figured he'd at least try to keep Kenny away as much as possible. "It's a friend of mine who needed the help at his garage—I owe him a favor, so Kenny's been making good on it for me."

Cools got it. Times were tough everywhere, even in the extortion business.

"Glad you're keeping your nose clean, kid. The last thing we need is for the military to be up our ass."

Cools had been a Marine and gotten honorably discharged after taking shrapnel to the thigh and arm. The scars on both were bad, but he could still move and he was built like a bull.

Jace thought he was probably the most mentally balanced of all the members, not that that was saying much.

Still, it could always be worse. He'd learned that a long time ago, and he realized it still held true when Cools ushered Jace into the main room where the others—including Kenny—were gathered for a meeting. Jace usually wasn't privy to this, for his own safety, but today it looked like that didn't matter.

Hopefully, he'd get some firsthand intel that would ultimately help the Feds help Kenny, because this was getting to be too dangerous.

You could always ask Clint...

He pushed that thought from his mind, refusing to let any of this blow back on Clint. The Feds thought Tomcat was dead and were using intel Kenny gave on him to take down the MC. Involving the dead man would prove too risky for Clint— because if the MC ever found out about him, forget it.

"We've got a rat," Cools announced finally, after closing the door. "And I'm gonna snap his neck."

Instinctively, Kenny moved closer to Jace. To an outsider, it would've looked like protectiveness, but in reality, it was the other way around.

Cools glared at Kenny, and Jace cursed silently, willing himself not to move a muscle.

"What happened?" one of the newer guys called, saving the situation, because Cools walked to him promptly and punched him out.

Yeah, regular question-and-answer sessions didn't happen in a place like this. Here, arcane caveman law applied, where it was all about survival and climbing the ranks, drinking and fucking as much as possible while trying to kill more than the other guy.

Now, Jace waited, so tense he could break, for the other shoe to drop. From what he understood of Tomcat's mission, it included a bit of backstabbing to confuse the men and turn them against one another. The CIA had wanted so much internal confusion that the MC didn't notice the bust coming.

If they pulled this off, it would be the largest bust in DEA history, and it would send a huge message to the MCs, and it still wouldn't make a dent, Clint had said.

"Then why bother?" Jace had asked.

"You have to try. You can't let the bastards win."

"Kenny, you look nervous," Cools said now.

"I don't like it when we don't stick together." And that was pure Kenny—his honesty had gotten him out of more than a few scrapes.

Cools snorted. "Think how much I don't like it."

Jace hoped it was enough to get Kenny off the hook. No matter what or who they were punishing, Jace wouldn't be involved. But his cousin would have to see and hear everything in excruciating detail, and MC guys could get very creative in the ways they doled out pain and punishment, thanks to their military backgrounds.

"No offense, Jace, but this is where you exit. I think, for a while, you should probably keep your nose out of club business. It'd be better for you and for Kenny—but I wanted you to hear the reason in person. It's a mutual club decision. We cool?"

"Yeah, got it." Jace clamped a hand on Kenny's shoulder, shook Cools's hand and prayed Kenny didn't fuck this up and remembered all the details discussed. It was too damned risky to wire his cousin under these circumstances, when they were already on edge and looking for a reason to hurt someone.

As he exited, he noted that Nacho and Shaz were missing from the meeting, which was unusual, especially since they weren't on guard duty outside the building.

He found them in the alley outside the club when they jumped him. He held them off as best he could without fighting, because his hands were considered deadly weapons. So he took more shots than he should've before he finally subdued them.

"Did Cools send you to do this?" he demanded.

"We heard from a source that you were the rat," Nacho moaned through his split lip. "Got a phone call that Shaz and I should take care of it ourselves."

"Who called you?"

"Some dude—didn't get his name. Fuck, Jace, we shouldn't have jumped so quick, but you gotta understand, everything's fucked around here."

Yeah, it was. He took the pressure off Nacho's neck and helped the man up. Shaz was starting to come to. "I won't tell Cools if you won't."

"Deal." Nacho stuck his hand out.

"And leave my cousin alone—he's too stupid to be the rat."

"He *is* kinda stupid, Jace," Nacho said.

Yeah, and you're a fucking brain trust. "Just get inside and stay out of my way."

The men slunk away, back to the door they were supposed to be guarding, and Jace walked to his bike, ignoring the pain of being rolled. His ribs were bruised, not broken—he knew from experience—but they still hurt like a bitch.

When his phone rang, he knew Jack's number immediately. His gut tightened, and before he answered, he put a GPS on the guy's number, because the guy wasn't as good as he thought.

195

"You shouldn't have done that," Jace said, not bothering to hear what Jack had to say.

"Clint's been in my life a lot longer than yours. I already told you, he's going to get sick of you. He always does. This is his MO—he always comes back to me. Always."

As Jack spoke, Jace triangulated his location, a couple of blocks away. Even before Jack admitted it, Jace knew he'd been the one who'd sold him out to the club. And now the asshole was going to pay for fucking with him and his family.

Jack had to know Jace would be coming for him. It was probably what he wanted, but Jace was too goddamned angry to care.

The guy was fucking with him, taunting him. And halfway to Jack's, Jace realized that confronting the asshole wasn't the way to go, at least not tonight. He wouldn't be able to control himself, and with Jace's luck, Jack would get him arrested.

Instead, he backtracked to the MC to grab Kenny and realized that Jack had set his cousin up as effectively as he had Jace.

Cools had beat the shit out of Kenny and left him alone on the floor. Jace hauled him to the ER, where he'd stay overnight due to a concussion and broken ribs.

Two others in the MC had also been killed night before last, a deal gone bad. Part of Tomcat's plan had been to plant intel that caused confusion among the ranks, forcing the men to turn on one another, while letting the CIA and DEA use the information gathered to make the larger bust. It was going along great, but not for Kenny or Jace, by extension, and Jack's interference hadn't helped.

Since the Feds were less than helpful, Jace made a few calls to some former team members doing black ops around the country and finally settled on sending Kenny to Montana instead of the Omaha group he'd originally considered. He didn't want to involve anyone in his cousin's stupidity, but there were two retired Marines who ran a snow removal business who could give Kenny room and board. There couldn't be a lot of gangs there, right? It would be a long, harsh winter, and Kenny could hole up. Jace had been saving for that eventuality for the past year.

He double-checked his bank account, and he had enough for a while. He could sell his place, too, take quarters on base.

"Hey, Kenny, I made some calls," he told his cousin, who was starting to stir.

"Jace, look...you're causing more trouble this way. I think...I want to stay in, all right? You're not in charge of me." Kenny was mumbling through painkillers, but his words had the ring of truth to them.

"I won't give up on you."

"I don't need you to watch me—I'm grown, man. Just go."

Utterly defeated and wondering why he didn't just give the hell up completely, Jace did as Kenny asked. Halfway to his bike, his phone buzzed—Clint's text. Obviously, Clint was home from his mission and wanted to meet up tonight. The timing couldn't have been goddamned worse, and so Jace typed with impatient, shaking fingers, *Can't make it tonight. Need to be alone.*

Harsh, but true. Even being tied down and fucked wouldn't help him tonight. He wasn't sure what would, but packing up and running away sounded really good right about now.

"Yeah, my cabin's free. Come by and grab the keys," Sawyer told him when he called. "I'd join you if Rex wasn't riding me."

"And not the way you want," Jace managed, and the two shared a short laugh.

SE Jakes

"Stay the week if you want."

Right, the doc had insisted Jace take that much time, since he'd worked with the guys who'd died. He thought about Kenny—maybe he should hang around town for him and try to convince him to go to Montana ASAP, but he knew that would be an uphill battle. And Jace was tired of doing what he was supposed to.

Jace wasn't home and he hadn't been answering his texts for the past twenty-four hours. When he finally did with a brush-off, Clint knew something was really wrong. Confirmed it when he spoke with his CIA handler, who told him that there'd been a fight at the MC.

"They jumped your boy. Didn't do much damage, but they beat the shit out of his cousin for good measure, just to make sure he's scared enough not to think about ratting."

"Why do they think either of them would?"

"No idea," his handler said. "But I'm looking into it."

Clint called Rex then, because he didn't have Sawyer's number. "Ask your boy where mine went."

Rex sighed. "He's not my goddamned boy, but I know where Jace is. I heard Sawyer telling him it was okay for him to use the cabin."

"Directions."

Rex rattled them off. It was only an hour's drive, and Clint was already in the car when he hung up with Rex.

Chapter Twenty-Six

Jace got to the cabin before midnight and ignored calls from the Feds and texts from Clint that implied the man knew about the fights Jace had gotten into with the MC. Fuck it. He turned his cell phone off, put his stuff away and sat on the screened porch with a beer until his eyes got heavy.

He woke with a start. Hadn't had this particular nightmare in ages, but being hit always brought it back.

Frankly, he was surprised the dream wasn't worse. But still, he was on the porch of Sawyer's cabin, breathing hard, covered in sweat and trembling. And the last person he expected to see when he opened his eyes was Clint, standing close enough for Jace to see the worry in his eyes.

"What the hell is going on?" Clint asked finally.

With the back of his hand, Jace wiped his brow and then his upper lip before downing the rest of the beer that had remained mercifully balanced and unspilled in his lap. He didn't know if he'd cried out in his sleep, but now he was embarrassed and pissed. "I didn't ask you to come here."

He hoped the lack of light left Clint unable to see the bruising on his face, but he doubted it. Knowing the man, he already had the full story before arriving.

"I came anyway."

SE Jakes

"You can go."

"I thought we had an understanding."

Jace could see that Clint was trying to hold back his anger and not succeeding.

"I thought I was allowed to have time to myself."

"You know I'm not talking about that, so don't even attempt to bullshit me. I told you to stay away from the MC. You said you would."

"I couldn't," Jace said flatly.

"You could've been killed."

"I don't deal in what-ifs."

"How very military of you," Clint said dryly, looked at Jace's bruised cheek closely. "I want to kill the men who did this to you with my bare hands."

"It's nothing," he said in an attempt to cut off Clint's concerns at the pass.

"I wish it was."

"Clint, I get you're worried—I really do. But I can handle my own shit."

"So this happened because you were handling your own shit?"

"Actually, it happened because of Jack, since you want to know so damned badly."

"Jack had something to do with this?" Clint asked, and Jace nodded. "You're sure?"

"Considering he told me, yeah, I'm pretty damned sure."

"I'll kill him."

"I almost took care of that myself, but it's not worth it, Clint."

"It is if he's fucking with your life."

200

"I can take care of shit myself."

"I realize that, but I want to help you."

"I didn't need help."

Clint sighed. "Why do you keep trying to push me away?"

Jace wanted to say he didn't know, but he did. And he was tired of being sorry for things. So he didn't say a word.

"Do you really not want me here?" Clint asked, his tone softer now.

"I need...time."

"Not sex. I know. But you shouldn't be alone, and I'm not leaving." He moved away from Jace and went into the house with his bag. Came back out and grabbed groceries from his truck, and within ten minutes of him going inside, Jace smelled food cooking. And still, he stayed outside for another hour until the alcohol worked and the tension left his body.

"Eat, then sleep," Clint told him when he brought him out a giant dish of stew and fresh bread. Clint didn't stay out there with him, and when Jace came in, he noted that Clint had taken the second bedroom.

He didn't know why that pissed him off, but it did. At the very least, Clint had respected his wishes in that small way, and Jace hadn't wanted him to. Not right now, when he was calmer and hurting and wanting Clint to work his magic.

And that wasn't fair to the man, either. He'd acted like an asshole, and it had nothing to do with the fact that Clint tracked him down.

He wasn't big on apologies, but he had to do something. So he stood in the small hallway where he knew Clint could see him, and he stripped down, slowly. Knew Clint was watching him but didn't make eye contact. Leaned against the wall and stroked his cock. He closed his eyes and let out a long, low

SE Jakes

moan, and he heard Clint's breathing quicken.

"I need you," he said finally, a whisper so low he wasn't sure he'd even spoken out loud. But he didn't need to open his eyes to feel Clint in front of him. The man's hands slowly took his shoulders, pulled him close, stopping him from stroking long enough to put his hands around Clint's back.

They stood there together in the quiet, his heart pounding against Clint's, and he didn't know what to say.

Luckily, Clint didn't seem to need to hear anything, just told Jace, "Put your hands above your head," and when Jace complied, Clint left him there for a second and returned with lube. He began to stroke Jace's ass as he moaned, and then he let go of Jace's arms and warned, "You'd better hold on."

Jace climbed the man, his arms and legs twined around him, and Clint entered him in one long stroke. The way he was positioned, his legs were spread so wide that the pain quickly turned to pleasure as Clint's cock speared his prostate over and over and he was thrusting back as best he could, his moans uncontrollable.

He'd thought he wouldn't be up for sex that night. But it seemed to be exactly what he needed to start healing.

No, you needed Clint. And that was the bottom line. It scared him more than anything.

"I'm glad you tracked me down," he said when they were done, after Clint carried him back into one of the bedrooms—it didn't matter which one—and covered him.

"Always, baby. Because it's what you want, even when you think you don't."

The man knew him well, and Jace wanted so badly to confess everything to him. But that would change everything between them.

202

Are you ever going to tell him?

No. Not if he could help it.

Something was still bothering Jace. Clint stroked his hair, and he waited semipatiently until Jace finally said, "You know, I harp on you all the time about not opening up to me, but I haven't exactly been open with you all the time either."

"Why's that?"

"Probably because I hate talking about it. Maybe I think you'll think less of me. So by not coming out and telling you, I've been covering my own six."

"Nice armchair psychology," Clint said. "While you share, will you let me clean some of those scrapes up?"

Jace sighed, fake-dramatic. "Fine."

Clint got the supplies he needed, plus ice, and went to work while Jace sat patiently. Clint could tell that he wanted to open up but was unsure of where to begin.

"Did you grow up with Kenny?" he asked.

"Yeah. When my parents died, Kenny's parents raised me. They were older when they had him, and so Kenny and I are all we have left." Jace paused. "The weird thing is, we aren't close—not the same interests or friends or ambitions, but I'd do anything for him."

Clint wanted to tell Jace if that were true, he should be getting them both out of the MC, but he refrained. "You enlisted right out of high school?"

"Yeah, couldn't wait. My grades sucked. I hated school, didn't like it until I knew what I wanted to do, and then all the pieces fit."

"You decided on the teams?"

"More like they picked me. I was headed into the pilot

203

program. My CO tossed out a challenge and here I am. Never could resist a challenge."

Clint felt a sense of unease settle in his gut. Was he just one more challenge in Jace's life? If so, well, hell, he'd been more than halfway conquered.

But domesticated? He looked around, and fuck, next he'd be doing the kid's laundry.

"What about you? Military in your family?" Jace was asking him.

"My grandfather," Clint confirmed "My dad was in the CIA. I was used to being alone."

"You're an only child?"

"Yes."

Jace looked at him strangely for a second, and Clint tensed, waited for the inevitable questions. Instead, Jace opened up his own floodgates. "My childhood sucked. Would've been worse if my mom hadn't died of alcohol poisoning and my dad in a drunken wreck before I went to live with Kenny's family," Jace said roughly, hating to have to revisit this, and knowing it was necessary.

Clint was silent for a long moment, his hand still on Jace's shoulder, and he knew the man was looking at the markings on his back in a different light. "I don't want to make a big fucking deal about it," he added.

"Some of these scars, then..." Clint trailed off as his fingers moved over puckered skin, but his tone of voice hadn't changed any—there wasn't pity—just questions.

"He was always careful to keep the bruises out of sight," Jace explained.

His eyes met Clint's, and he saw the anger, carefully

controlled but right under the surface. This man would kill for him—save him—do anything for him if and when Jace asked, and maybe sometimes when he didn't. It hadn't become that clear, that simple, until that moment.

It panicked him more than it should have. Instead of focusing on why, he answered Clint's unspoken question.

"I probably would've gotten to that point myself. I shot up enough that next year after he died. I always wonder if he would've kept fucking with me if I was bigger."

"Bullies always think they're bigger," Clint said. "What the hell could you have done?"

"He found out I wasn't his. My mom had an affair. He took it out on us, and she took it out on me." His tears rose hotly to the surface, but he held them back. They didn't deserve them—never had. "Childhood really sucked. But it evened out a little when I got to Kenny's. His parents expected me to keep an eye on him, and I did."

It was a perfect time to confess everything, but when Clint pulled him in for a kiss, he wanted that way more.

"You're still upset. Talk to me, Jace. You want me to stop holding back, so you stop, too."

Clint looked so earnest, and Jace wanted to just fuck the man—or be fucked. Wanted the talking to stop immediately.

"When I have shit to deal with—"

"You run. And by run, I mean avoid—like the hotel in Stan. After the SEALs were killed. This..."

Jace glared at him, but his mouth finally twisted into a wry grin. "Yeah, all right—I get it. So, what do you do when you have shit to deal with?"

"Chase me and find out."

"I did, remember? That first night."

"I recall inviting you in—taking you to the loft."

"Yeah, you did." Jace put his head against Clint's shoulder. "I wouldn't have let you get hurt that night."

"Why are you surprised when I feel the same?"

Jace shrugged. "I haven't had too many people in my life who have. I figured, don't get used to things. Makes it easier."

"But you care about Kenny—won't leave him behind."

"Yeah, well, he's not very street smart. Got involved with the Killers before I knew. I never would've let him join."

Clint held him closer. "We'll figure it out."

"I hope so." Jace really wasn't sure at all. He'd blown the Feds off and would probably get his ass handed to him. But he hadn't betrayed a single confidence of Clint's. "Sometimes it's all so hard. Sometimes, I just want easy."

"You know as well as I do that the things worth having are those you fought the hardest for."

"I fought battles because I refused to let anyone get bullied or hurt around me," Jace said fiercely. "I probably did too much."

"You can never do too much," Clint said quietly.

"You were abused?"

"Not physically."

"Sometimes, the other kind is worse," Jace said. And then Clint sat there and told him about his father—his mother—a childhood that didn't resemble a childhood at all. And just like that, everything they'd done to each other made sense, the way Clint didn't think he could have a life outside the CIA, the way Jace ran when Clint was in danger of getting too close to him. The final pieces of the puzzle fit—and fit well. The walls were finally down, past laid out like scattered cards that needed to be put back into place, but it would be a new order. A stronger, better one.

Clint moved to dig in the pocket of his jacket, brought back a key. "I'll give you the code too. I don't spend a lot of time there because it's not a home. I like staying at your place. It feels right."

Jace stared at him, weighed his next words carefully. "Why don't you move in with me, then?"

"Just like that? What happens when you need your space?" Clint's voice was teasing but then he added, "I don't want to crowd you, but I'd like to come home to you—or you to me."

"I'd like that. I wouldn't have offered otherwise. I'm out of the MC."

"You're choice or the MC's?"

"Both," he admitted. "If I can't convince Kenny to get out of state, which is looking less and less likely, there's nothing more I can do. I've risked enough."

"Yeah, you have," Clint told him quietly. Jace took the key from him anyway, even though he wouldn't be needing it.

He'd tell his handler that he was done in the morning and let the chips fall where they may. And then he'd tell Clint. But not now—he wasn't ruining this.

Chapter Twenty-Seven

Rex was surprised to find Sawyer at his door. He'd been thinking about calling the boy, or going to his place, but instead he'd let them both go about their business like they were unaffected. The biggest lie he'd ever told himself, and he had to force himself to invite Sawyer in and stand in the living room instead of immediately dragging him up into the bedroom and never allowing him to leave again.

Sawyer shoved his hands in his pockets and asked, "Why don't you let me stay over?"

Rex looked into his eyes and admitted, "I have nightmares."

Sawyer swallowed hard, like he hadn't been sure at all of what Rex would say, and then he relaxed a little, even as Rex tensed up further. "Okay. Well, I think I can handle that."

Rex snorted. "I can't even handle them."

"Maybe if someone's with you when you sleep, they won't come," Sawyer said. "I'm guessing you never tried that."

"No, I haven't. I didn't want you to have to hear me wake up like that, all right? I can't control them. I fucking hate them."

"It's because of what happened—your capture, right?"

"Yeah." Rex shook his head. "I feel like I'll never get it out of my head. I've got to make it stop fucking with me."

"Talking about it's probably a good thing."

"Not sure how the hell you got so smart," Rex grumbled.

"Can I see the scars?"

Rex wanted to say no, but he couldn't. Sawyer wasn't going to let him off the hook that easily, and if roles were reversed, Rex wouldn't have either. Instead, he simply nodded and let Sawyer approach him.

The boy didn't hesitate, came close to him and circled around to his back. Kissed the side of his neck, and Rex closed his eyes and willed himself to let Sawyer do what he needed to.

First, Sawyer pulled his shirt off. Rex felt the cool air rake his warm skin, and as much as he wanted to turn around and not let Sawyer see any of these under the light of day, he knew he had to let the boy in all the way.

He'd made Sawyer let him in, yanked his walls down. It wouldn't be fair not to do the same.

Sawyer knew his struggle, because he said, "It's okay, Rex. Just me. I've seen them before—at least these," as his fingers trailed lightly over the scars on his back.

The team had all seen those particular scars—but the other ones, not so much. Rex was pretty sure that the shower had been dark enough on the night Sawyer watched him.

He wasn't a vain man at all—that wasn't what it was about. But the powerlessness he'd felt in that cell during the torture— that he couldn't shake.

When Sawyer reached around to unzip his jeans and finally pulled them down, Rex opened his eyes and stared at a fixed point the wall, even as he kicked the denim off and stood defiantly, arms crossed.

Sawyer's fingers trailed lower, and he sucked in a rough breath. "I never knew about these." His fingers went lower, almost reverently touching the marks on Rex's thighs. "What you survived..."

"It wasn't bad."

"Bullshit," Sawyer told him, then kissed along his shoulder. "This is you—me—no bullshit."

"Right." Rex did turn then and looked at Sawyer over his shoulder. "Don't you dare pity me."

"I was thinking about how much more I want you every day," Sawyer replied, and hell, Rex believed him. He turned, took Sawyer into his arms, grateful the man didn't make him feel any less of one.

"Do you get why I ride you so hard out of the bedroom now?"

Sawyer smiled. "Yeah, I do. I'm important to you."

"Damn right. And you're one of the best I've seen in a long time. You and Jace—you make a good team."

"I think we make a better one."

"Yeah, that." Rex touched the side of his face and smiled.

"I wasn't captured, so I can't say I understand," Sawyer started. "But when Jace and I were trapped in that cave, that feeling of *is this it?* can overwhelm you. We're taught to never think in terms of failure, and we didn't, but at some point you've still got to make your peace."

"What was yours?"

"To tell you how I felt," Sawyer said without hesitation.

"No shit?"

"No shit."

"Then what took you so long?"

"Because I don't just want sex, which must make me some kind of genetic freak because it's supposed to be the other way around for a guy," Sawyer said. "But I've seen this happen—I won't be the goddamned ghost. The back-up. The punching bag for when you realize I'm not and never will be Josh."

"Do you have that little faith in me? Or are you just scared?"

"The latter," Sawyer told him seriously.

"I've waited a long time for a new love, Sawyer. I didn't want a replacement for Josh—that wouldn't be fair to his memory either. I just...I didn't want to be hurt."

"I won't hurt you," the boy whispered. "If I thought I would, I'd never have started this. Never would've come to your door if I hadn't been ready."

"And if you thought I'd hurt you?"

"Don't, Rex." He spoke so plaintively that Rex knew he was never going to let this boy out of his life.

For a long while, Sawyer stood there in Rex's embrace. He was happy. Exhausted. And a little terrified.

"Who hurt you?" Rex finally asked him.

"Family. I watched what coming in behind the love of someone's life can do to someone," he admitted.

"I loved Josh, yes. But I can move on. Sometimes people can't. If I thought that...shit, I'd never have been drawn to you."

"Am I like him?"

Rex considered that. "Josh was older than me by a year. He was quiet. Serious."

"Sounds like you."

Rex laughed. "Yeah, he was."

Sawyer was the opposite of Rex. He was always in motion, although not frenetic. He was always planning.

"You're more stubborn. Competitive with yourself. Josh was easygoing."

"You liked that."

"Actually, it drove me fucking nuts a lot of the time," Rex said. "We were good together, but were far from the perfect couple."

"Would he be okay with this?"

"More than," Rex said.

"So what now?"

"We stay under the radar and make sure none of this affects our performance."

"Do you want me to transfer?"

"Hell no."

And just like that, Sawyer realized he'd finally lived up to the promise he'd made himself.

Chapter Twenty-Eight

As they lay there in a comfortable silence, Clint traced the track of a lazy figure eight down the boy's back, noting a new scar, no doubt from a recent mission. He rubbed it with his forefinger, knowing better than to ask but wanting to anyway.

"Never should've turned my back on that goddamned informant," Jace said, reading his mind. "But it was better than taking a round to the chest on that particular mission."

"Much," Clint agreed, replaced his finger with his tongue, running it down Jace's spine while the younger man moaned, because he knew where Clint was headed.

Jace buried his face in the pillow as Clint's tongue found its mark, licking, sucking, probing the tender skin before spearing and thrusting his tongue into Jace's hole, causing Jace to squirm and hump the bed.

Clint pulled his hips up, the Dom in him unable to resist torturing Jace with the best kind of pleasure, leaving Jace frustrated with his dick not able to gain the friction he sought.

But there was nothing he could do, not until Clint began to open him with his fingers and finally, his cock.

He pulled Jace up to kneel against him, his back to Clint's chest, and finally, he stroked Jace, letting the man come before he did. Murmured, "Love you," against the boy's neck when they were done, and Jace turned his head to stare at him.

It had come out so easily, there was no denying it. "I love you, Jace."

Jace blinked, muttered, "Holy shit."

"You don't have to say it back now."

"I didn't think *you'd* ever say it. I didn't want to bring it up and freak you out," Jace continued. "I think I've loved you since that first night."

Clint pulled him back down to the bed to enjoy the moment—perfect and drama free.

The next morning, while Jace was on the phone with Kenny, arguing, even pleading—all to no avail—Clint got a call that he was due on a plane in less than forty-eight. He watched Jace as he continued to talk on his own phone, and when the boy finally hung up, he looked a little shaken but at least at peace.

"It's done," he told Clint.

And for the next forty hours, Clint planned on making the most of their time together. "Do you need to get home or can we stay here?"

"Stay, definitely."

Clint tugged him into the bedroom and onto the mattress. Within minutes, he had Jace squirming under his touch.

"Please."

He didn't know if Jace was begging for more or more mercy, but Clint didn't plan on stopping anytime soon. Instead, he lifted Jace's hips so he could tug the boy against him, his cock hitting Jace's prostate over and over, which was why the boy was incoherent at the moment. His eyes were closed, head moving side to side, arms overhead with hands wrapped around the metal bar of the headboard.

Clint's balls tightened but he forced himself to wait. The cock ring he'd put on Jace was helping him, but he wanted to see, so he unwrapped it and Jace came immediately in hard spurts of white ropes that decorated his belly and chest and hit the wall, too.

"Beautiful," Clint murmured as he pumped into him while Jace rode out his orgasm. Afterward, Jace smiled up at him, his eyes hazy.

And then Jace pumped back up against Clint until he came in an earthshaking orgasm that made his body clench before he released, surprised he didn't blow the condom off.

He bent forward, propped over the boy on his elbows, refusing to pull out just yet.

"So fucking good," Jace murmured as he stroked Clint's back absently, his thighs trembling a little from having been held up and open for so long.

Clint dipped his head and licked Jace's nipple, and the boy shivered underneath him. "Glad you had a good time. But we're far from done."

"Mmmmm." Jace was falling asleep, his feet rubbing Clint's, the soft bed and Clint's warm body rocking him.

Jace hadn't thought this part would ever be as good as it was, lying here, trapped, held, not wanting to move at all.

Damn, he could get used to this.

Damn, he already was.

"Your stomach's growling," Clint said. "Let me make you something."

"You just want to keep my energy up so you can fuck me again."

"Absolutely." Clint finally pulled out of him, and Jace

215

winced. He was already sore. "I'll fix that."

"'S'all right," he protested, even as Clint ran him a bath and had him sit for a while, then he came and dried him, fed him and tucked him back into bed, satiated.

When he woke, it was the next morning, and Clint was pressed to him, and they were both hard.

Clint's hand reached around and stroked him, and they rocked against one another until they both climaxed.

After a shower and breakfast, they lay around and watched movies.

"I never do this," Jace said, punctuated it with a low, jaw-cracking yawn. He was stretched out along one couch, Clint the other, and they'd barely moved.

"You need to do it more."

"Who are you kidding? You never do this either."

"Then we need to do it together more."

Jace shifted and winced. "Yeah, because we're not having sex anytime soon."

"There are plenty of other things we can do," Clint told him. "Just you wait."

Jace wasn't disappointed. Clint was pretty damned creative. And when Jace finally got the nerve, that night, to broach the subject he'd been curious about, well, he was pretty shocked at the response.

"You want to fuck me, pretty baby?" Clint practically crooned, and Jace bit his lip and nodded.

"Nobody's stopping you."

Jace let out the breath he'd been holding as Clint leaned

back on his elbows and waited for Jace to take the reins.

He wasn't sure where he wanted to start, because he wanted to make Clint feel as good as the man always made him feel. And Clint was surprisingly patient, considering the man was for sure a top.

"I'll help." Clint urged him forward.

"I feel like a virgin again."

"You and me both," Clint told him. "It's been a long time for me."

"You don't like it?"

"Has to be the right person. With you, it'll be good."

That was all Jace needed to hear, and he blocked out the question he most wanted answered in favor of moving forward. He leaned in and began to kiss Clint as the man relaxed and lay back. He kissed his way down Clint's body, licking, sucking, ending up with his mouth on Clint's dick as Clint's hands pushed through his hair, and he said Jace's name in a tense whisper.

Jace moved farther down and held Clint's legs open, began to rim him until the man was half jelly and a whimpering mess. And finally, Jace was opening him with fingers, slowly, working Clint through the tension of being invaded.

"You ready?"

Clint nodded, the trust in his eyes unmistakable. "Go ahead. And, for the record, not with Jack. Never."

"Good." Jace positioned himself between Clint's legs. He knew the man probably would rather be on his hands and knees, a less vulnerable position, but he was doing this for Jace. Now, Jace entered him, his cock breaching the first ring of muscle as he watched the mix of emotions on Clint's face.

"Come on, man—don't baby me," Clint urged, and Jace

217

pushed in all the way, hard and fast but still holding back slightly.

But Clint loved it, arched his back and met Jace's cock with a push of his own. Wanted to keep moving, but Jace refused, asking instead, "How long?"

"Years," Clint managed. "Ten. Or more. Some of my first times with no one that mattered. This matters. Fucking move, Jace—please."

To hear Clint beg made Jace want to burst with pleasure—he almost came right then and there, but he held on and he moved the way Clint wanted, fucked him until he heard the big man whimper, and he knew he was hitting the right place.

When Clint came, sticky between their bellies, Jace didn't stop, rode Clint through his orgasm before he allowed himself to spiral out of control. When he did pump inside Clint, he wasn't sure what he said—his words tumbled out in an incoherent rush.

He lay sprawled on Clint, aware his body was probably a dead weight. But Clint didn't complain—instead he rubbed Jace's back slowly.

"You're still hard," Clint whispered. "Damned youth."

"What's your excuse?" Jace asked.

"Motherfucker," Clint said, and Jace found himself flipped so he was on his back, legs spread with Clint inside him.

Jace hadn't been sure he was capable of any more orgasms, but man, did he feel good, couldn't remember the last time he was more relaxed. He lay on fresh sheets next to Clint as a movie rolled.

He'd gotten plenty of sleep, so he wasn't worried that it was late. He'd drift off eventually, and then he probably wouldn't see

Clint again for months. Clint was leaving this time, but Jace would leave again soon, too, and his trips tended to last longer than Clint's.

"I'll wait," Clint said.

"I didn't realize I spoke out loud."

"You didn't, but you go tense all of a sudden. And since I leave in six hours—it's a natural assumption that you're thinking about us being separated again. What'll happen afterward."

Jace stared at him. "I'll wait, too. You know that."

"Let's try to make it under six months."

"And if it's not?"

"I'll still wait," Clint said quietly.

Chapter Twenty-Nine

Styx was in town for the day, and he met Clint at Jace's house—although technically, Clint had moved in and never looked back. Jace had made him keys and said nothing when all Clint's belongings began showing up in the house, in the closets and the kitchen. Said nothing when Clint began parking in the driveway.

"So you're living together?" Styx asked mildly.

"I'm never home, so this was just easier," Clint explained, but he knew that wasn't it at all.

"You're really in deep." Styx leaned back with a small smirk.

"You're enjoying that a little too much."

Styx looked out the window—Law and Paulo had just pulled up. The three of them had been making their relationship work for a year now—as unconventional as it was, it was perfect for them. For Damon and Tanner, too, although he knew Damon worried about Tanner on his boy's long missions away.

"You could both get out—work black ops together, if that's what turns you both on," Styx suggested. "Because you're mooning around without him. "

Clint threw the empty soda can at Styx's head. The man

ducked and shook his head. "Man, you've got it bad."

"Let's just go with your boys to lunch, all right?"

Styx didn't argue, but Clint knew it wasn't the end of the conversation.

He'd been right, of course, but they gave him until after the meal was finished and they waited on coffee before really digging in.

Law threw out the first casual blow. "Business is really heating up—we could use a few more guys. Know anyone who'd be interested?"

"Subtle as shit, Law," Paulo told his lover. "Just ask him."

"I think you just did," Styx pointed out.

Clint caught the way these men looked at one another—a combination of respect and love that couldn't be faked, and man, they were lucky.

Maybe it was time for him to be lucky as well.

When Clint returned home hours later, the house was still empty. He checked his texts and there was nothing. He returned a call to his handler and got the man's voicemail, and then he sat for a while and pondered the offer Styx and Law and Paulo had made him.

He'd always known that door was open to him, but they'd extended it to Jace as well. And for the first time in forever, Clint was willing to take this leap with Jace. He'd meant it when he'd told him so months ago, but he realized Jace might not be ready yet. He'd only been with the SEALs for six years, and getting out now would be difficult.

But Clint still planned on talking this through with the boy when he came home.

He'd started making something for dinner, since there was only so much takeout a guy could have, when he heard the door open. He walked into the hallway to see Jace come in, shoulders looking like they were in knots, face drawn with exhaustion. But he smiled when he saw Clint, and they kissed with the deep appreciation that only being alive—being survivors—could give them. Jace dropped his bag and hung on to Clint, and he knew if he let the boy have his way, they'd be fucking right here in the hallway. And after a couple months apart, it was definitely something that topped Clint's list, but making sure Jace was all right came higher.

He pulled away, but Jace kept his hand on the back of his neck. "What's wrong?"

"You." Clint steered him upstairs toward the bedroom.

"I'm fine," Jace protested.

"I'll be the judge of that," Clint told him. "Let's clean you up, get food into you. Then sleep and sex."

"Sex, then sleep," Jace said. "Maybe a shower first."

"I'm more than glad to assist."

He embraced the boy, felt the rough equipment Jace used, and then began to peel away the layers of the boy's uniform carefully, piece by piece, until they were down to bare, albeit sandy skin.

Clint swore he could tell where Jace had been based on that clue alone, but he didn't bother to ask. It didn't matter. What did was that Jace was back and here, in his arms.

Still, Clint bit back anger at the contusions littering Jace's chest and shoulders. Part of the job, the mission.

"I've already had medical treatment," Jace said as if to stave off further inspection. "It's nothing that won't heal."

Still, Clint traced a new knot in the boy's back—he'd always had scars, but seeing the active markings made Clint realize how close he came to losing this man every time they left each other.

"I know. I've seen your grave," Jace said quietly, reading Clint's thoughts. "Price of the job, right?"

Clint leaned in and kissed him fiercely. "Doesn't mean I have to like it."

Jace fought the process a little but complied after Clint said, "Let me," and prepped him for the shower so he could clean off the heat of the battle. Cleaning the memories of it away wouldn't be that easy, but his boy was better able to handle what was happening both between them and in his professional life than he'd been months earlier.

He led Jace to the shower and massaged his shoulders lightly while the water heated, then stripped and got them both inside the large, clear glass-enclosed stall.

He'd watched Jace in here more times than he could count—it never failed to pull him inside, no matter how clean he already was.

This time, he carefully soaped the boy up, washed his hair and then took down the waterproof lube and worked his fingers against Jace's ass as the boy groaned a little.

"Hang on to the towel rack," he urged, and Jace did so, holding so tightly his knuckles whitened. "Maybe I should cuff you in here," he continued as he pressed a slick finger inside of Jace as deeply as he could, and whether it was the words or the penetration that caused him to jump, Clint wasn't sure.

But he was far from done. It was two fingers and then three, all while he talked dirty and watched Jace's cock drip as the hot water bore down on them.

"Am I clean yet?" Jace asked finally, his voice slightly strangled.

SE Jakes

"Enough for me to start getting you dirty." He pushed Jace to the wall and entered him in one stroke, loving the way Jace took all of him with a cry of pleasure and Clint's name on his lips.

"Missed. You," Clint said along with his thrusts. "Missed. This."

Jace nodded in agreement, his palms trying to gain quarter against the slick tile, his body rigid with pleasure.

"Come on, baby, let me see you come," Clint told him, and Jace tensed and shot, come spurting up his stomach and chest.

Clint didn't last much longer, saw stars as Jace's tight ass contracted around him. He leaned his face into Jace's wet back as the shower beat down around them, and when he could move again, he cleaned them off, then toweled Jace dry and tucked him into bed, because he was already half-asleep.

"I'm going to wake you up to eat, all right?" he whispered, and Jace nodded before closing his eyes completely.

Clint suspected that would happen, and he figured an hour would be more than enough time for him.

He dried himself the rest of the way off, tugged on a pair of jeans and went into the kitchen, finished the prep for the meal. He was about to wake Jace up when the phone rang.

"Hey, got some of the intel you asked about." It was his supervisor, Pete, from the MC op, which was still in the process of wrapping up. The bust was happening soon, but it would be timed carefully.

"Tell me."

"Jace is being watched over by the Feds."

Pete's words stopped him cold. "He's in trouble?"

"The opposite—Jace is working with them."

"For how long?"

"Coupla years. It's some deal to get his cousin into WITSEC."

Clint glanced at the kitchen door and saw Jace ambling sleepily down the stairs, sweats sitting low on his hips.

"Thanks for the intel, man. Gotta run."

He managed to put the phone down rather than smash it against the wall the way he wanted to.

"Sleep well?"

Jace nodded as he rubbed his eyes with his palms. "Needed that."

"Bet you did." He couldn't do this, sit through dinner and pretend nothing was wrong. If it was an op, yes, but this was as far from it as it could be.

"What's wrong? Was that work?" Jace read his body language instantly.

"It was." He paused. "Want to tell me about your work with the Feds?"

"The Joint Commission?"

"No, the Feds who promised Kenny protection if you cooperated and agreed to spy on the MC in return."

Jace stared at him, neither confirming nor denying, but he paled a little and muttered, "Shit."

"You didn't think I'd find out?"

"I didn't...look, I never asked you for any favors, did I?"

"That's not what this is about, and you know it." Clint heard his own voice, dangerously low, and Jace's stance mirrored that, was equally as tense.

"It was something I started before you and I had to finish it. And I did finish it. I got out."

"Without telling me?"

"Yes." Jace stood firm, and Clint did throw the phone to the wall across from Jace, watched it smash into a million pieces.

"Why the hell not, Jace? And don't tell me you forgot for a fucking year or couldn't find the time or whatever other bullshit you're going to justify this with."

"Because you'd worry. And you'd try to fix it, and I don't drag people into my problems."

"Suppose I want to be dragged there? Don't I get a say?"

"I didn't want to blow your cover. Don't you get it? The Feds think you were really killed. You could've gotten in deep shit with the CIA for being with me—you told me that yourself. I didn't want there to be a hint of impropriety. And the Feds threatened me. Once I refused to give them any more intel and Kenny refused to leave town, I knew they could screw me. Big time. And I've been waiting for that shoe to drop."

Clint paused at that, but he was too angry to look at it rationally. He was too pissed and this was too personal. "You could've really fucked with my op."

"I just pointed that out," Jace told him. "I haven't used a single thing you told me. You can check with my handler. I'd never do anything to hurt you, on or off the job."

"You just did, so how can I believe anything you say?"

"You seriously believe I'd use you for intel?"

"I think you'd use intel I had to get Kenny help. And I told you things."

"I never asked—you told me to try to get out."

"And you fed that intel—"

"I got that intel about the bust on the warehouse on my own, months before I left. Months before we slept together. The Feds waited too long to move on the warehouse intel. Check the dates if you want."

"I will. And it was a stupid goddamned plan to ask the Feds to help you," Clint continued.

"It's none of your business," Jace countered.

"Everything you do is my business," he roared.

"Is everything you do my business?" Jace demanded. "Because I don't understand your ever-changing rules that only seem to suit you and your needs."

"Yeah, like switching subjects is going to throw me off the track," Clint said. "You're working with the Feds, and they don't give a shit about you or your cousin."

"I *was* working with them," Jace corrected. "I don't need protection."

"Yes, you do. You have no idea."

"I have every idea. I didn't go into this lightly." Jace yanked a shirt on.

"Right. You know what you're doing. And when Kenny disappears and the club gets screwed and you disappear, they won't make a connection?"

"I won't disappear."

"You're either stubborn or stupid."

"I'm not going to stand here and justify what I've done to you. I don't know what your fucking problem really is—"

"You weren't honest."

"Don't even fucking go there," Jace shouted. "I had my reasons."

"Not to trust me?"

"It's not about that."

Clint wasn't really sure what made him angrier, the fact that Jace was in danger or the Fed thing, but he was in no state of mind to untangle it now.

"I didn't tell anyone, not even Sawyer, and he and I almost goddamned died together, okay?"

"That's supposed to make it all right?"

"If I knew how to do that, I would've." Jace was breathing hard—emotion, not exertion, and Clint wanted to go to him and kiss the hurt away.

But, like always, and now more than ever, there was too much between them. A mountain to climb, and Clint was standing at the bottom looking up, and it was too damned high this time.

"You made your choice," Clint said.

"I made several choices, all of them to keep the people I love safe," Jace countered.

"Don't you dare bring love into this," Clint told him, wasn't surprised when Jace threw the first punch.

It was a physical fight in which there would be no winner. And although both knew that they'd lose, no matter what, they couldn't stop, not until they were both panting and angrier than they were when they started.

Finally, they stumbled away from each other, pissed and stunned and hurt. Jace's lip was bleeding, and Clint wanted to reach out and cradle him, tell him he was sorry, but he couldn't. The walls had gone back up hard, and the trust that had built up was smashed.

Jace shook his head, spat blood on the floor. "Fuck you for not trusting me."

"Right back at you."

"I couldn't risk Kenny's life."

"But you could risk mine?"

"I would never have let anything happen to you."

"Yeah, right." Clint's laugh was harsh. "You made your

choice before we got together. I don't blame you for choosing family over me, but I do blame you for not trusting me enough to tell me."

"If you believe that, we never had anything at all." Jace's face looked like stone, his voice hollow.

"My ass is on the line—literally!" Clint roared. "And if you fucked up what I spent years doing—"

"I would never do that."

"I don't believe you."

Jace seemed to sag a little at his words, like he'd been hit with a physical blow. But he regained his composure quickly. "The intel I gave the Feds about the warehouse and the Colombians—"

"Was exactly what I was dealing with—what I had the CIA take care of. Exactly what I told you," Clint finished.

"After the fact, Clint—you told me after you rose from the goddamned dead, okay? And I knew it months before you told me—before we slept together. I told you—I knew about the warehouse before you did. I figured out later on that it was part of your plan—the reason Tomcat died. I assumed you had undercovers in place—new ones—and I haven't said a goddamned word to the Feds about the new warehouse. That could've gotten Kenny into WITSEC and me off the hook months ago. But I said nothing."

Dammit, Clint wanted to believe him, but the boy said he would've done anything to keep his cousin safe.

He kept you safe, too.

And he just might be the reason you lose your entire career.

He didn't know what to believe, but he did realize that he didn't want to do any more damage. Instead, he grabbed as much of his gear as he could manage and got into his car and drove to the nearest hotel.

Jace called but he ignored the message. Didn't ignore the one from his supervisor that came in around three in the morning.

"Got a job and a jet waiting."

"I'll be on it," Clint assured him.

Before Clint boarded, he erased Jace's message without listening to it. And he wasn't sure which one of them was being more stubborn.

Chapter Thirty

Several weeks passed with no word from Clint, but when his phone rang in the middle of the night, Jace dove for it. But instead of Clint finally answering a call, it was Kenny—and Jace was his one phone call.

Now, Jace's hands shook on the wheel as he drove to the station, the phone on speaker and ringing endlessly.

"This better be good," he said when he picked up his old Fed handler's call.

"Heard Kenny's been arrested."

"You heard right. It's not your problem anymore."

"That's where you're wrong, Jace. Someone else got involved and tipped the MC off—the whole deal was almost blown."

Jace immediately suspected the CIA or the DEA, wondered if his handler did as well. "Like I said, it's not my problem."

"But it will be. If the MC thinks Kenny's selling them out, they'll kill him."

Jace knew that. Whenever the FBI or DEA used informants, they protected them as much as possible, arrested them when they did sweeps so as to stave off suspicion. So the fact that Kenny was arrested didn't take him off the MC's shit list. It might've put him right at the top of the list.

Jace hung up on him and drove at top speed to the police station. He didn't think Clint would do anything purposely to fuck up things with Kenny, but now Kenny was left hanging in the wind, and Jace was left with nothing. Literally, since Clint had walked out and refused to talk to him.

Clint watched Jace and Kenny leave the police station together. Kenny was the last of the Killers bailed out—the cops considered him a weak link and so they'd kept him and interrogated him for twenty-four hours straight. Jace was there for half of it—Clint watched him walk outside sometimes, pacing in the cold air, hands in his pockets, and he could see the frustration and worry in Jace's shoulders.

In the past, he'd have been the one to smooth that away, to take care of the rough edges. Hell, if Jace had admitted everything, Clint would've taken care of every goddamned thing for him, including the Kenny debacle.

And still, he couldn't let Jace take all the blame, because Jack had gotten involved where he shouldn't have and fucked all of this up. Throwing away a brilliant CIA career because what—he thought he loved Clint?

It was pure fucking jealousy, and there was nothing to do with love involved.

"I think they need protection," Clint said as Jace and Kenny wove through the parking lot.

"We've had someone on Jace's car the whole night," Pete pointed out.

Clint turned his binoculars on the several members of the MC who were waiting for them, to ensure Kenny hadn't said anything. Or maybe to take both men away where they'd never be heard from again.

Clint's gut tightened as he watched Jace approach the men.

"We're in position, Clint—nothing will happen."

Clint didn't believe it entirely, but he was relieved when Jace shook Cools's hand, and then he and Kenny got into a waiting, already-running car. Jace had obviously been worried about a car bomb, and he'd called a friend to pick them up. With the binoculars again, he noted it was Sawyer—along with Rex—and he heaved a small sigh of relief as it sped away into the night.

The MC cars and bikes went in the other direction.

"Are you going to tell him you saved his ass by letting the MC know that Kenny's not the rat?" Pete asked.

Clint shook his head. "Jace would never forgive me—he might not even believe me."

"Like he was going to do either one anyway?"

Clint shot Pete a look. "I don't expect you to get it."

"And I never expected you to have a relationship in the middle of an op."

"I've asked for one favor in all these damned years—"

"And I'm never going to let you forget it," Pete told him without rancor. "You're really not going to talk to him again?"

"Not now, anyway." Clint checked his ringing phone, which was surely another mission. "I'm going to be busy for a while."

"I'll get you to the airstrip," Pete told him, and Clint nodded and pretended he wasn't breaking apart inside.

Chapter Thirty-One

A month passed with no word from Clint. Jace waited as long as he could before dialing the special service Clint set up for them.

Two days and still nothing.

I'll never ignore this number, no matter what the hell is happening between us.

"You ever going to tell me what's wrong?" Sawyer asked him now. Jace had been so deep in his reverie, he hadn't noticed the company, which wasn't exactly the best thing to happen to a special forces operator.

"Clint."

"I figured that," Sawyer said. "He's been gone a while?"

"We had a fight," Jace told Sawyer. "And now he's not answering the number he gave me. He said he always would. I know he's pissed but—"

"Maybe he can't answer," Sawyer said bluntly, voicing the very thing Jace had refused to let himself think about.

Now he knew he couldn't ignore it any longer, not when his gut was screaming. "Fuck, I think you're right."

"What now? You can't exactly call the CIA."

"No, but I can do the next best thing." Jace scrolled through his phone, looking for the number for Clint's former

CIA partner, given to him in case Jace ran into an emergency.

Jace dialed it, figured it must've been a flagged line because the guy he assumed to be Styx answered before the second ring.

"Who the hell is this?"

"Is this Styx?"

A long pause that oozed suspicion. "Who the fuck is this?"

"It's Jace. I'm—"

"I know who you are," Styx said, the suspicion gone. "Are you in trouble?"

"Not me. I think Clint might be."

"Tell me what you know."

Shit, and this was where it would get embarrassing, but he could survive a little humiliation if he knew Clint was all right. "I, ah, he's not answering his phone. Not returning my calls."

Styx didn't say a word, and Jace squeezed his eyes closed and realized how goddamned desperately worried he actually was. Sawyer's hand clamped on his shoulder, like his friend was giving over his strength to Jace, which he appreciated.

"He's missing," Jace said.

"This has happened before," Styx said.

"And he told me it would never happen again," Jace said as if he was talking to a small, slow child. "Which is why I'm telling you that he's in danger. I'll call in my resources if I have to, but I'm hoping you can be of some goddamned assistance."

"You're going to have to give me more than that if I'm supposed to start an all-out manhunt for an undercover CIA operative on a top-secret mission, hear?" Styx told him.

Put up or shut up time. "Look, he gave me this special number—a service—and he told me he would always get back to me if I called it. And it's been a month since we talked and we had a fight, but I know something's wrong. And if you can't help me, I'll fucking find him myself."

"Calm down, Jace. I trust your instincts—and Clint told me about the number. I just needed you to tell me about it," Styx said. "Let me make some calls. Tell me your number, because it's blocked."

Jace rattled it off. "Thanks, Styx."

"We'll get to the bottom of it."

He hung up the phone and sat with Sawyer until the sun set along the beach. And still, the phone didn't ring.

The news wasn't good. Styx hung the phone up as Law stared at him from across the table, waiting for him to share.

Paulo stood in the doorway, semipatiently waiting as well.

"He's MIA," Styx said finally.

Law cursed and Paulo asked, "Where was he?"

"Afghanistan."

"I hope you've got a specific location," Law said.

"Is the CIA going to do anything?" Paulo demanded almost at the same time.

"Not yet," Styx said. "I'm going to have to go in after him and try not to fuck anything up."

"Not without us," Law told him. "And you're going to have a hell of a time holding Jace back too."

"I'm not taking that kid," Styx said.

"He'll go on his own and get hurt. Clint will never forgive you," Paulo said quietly, and Styx wondered yet again how the youngest member of their family always had the most goddamned wisdom.

Maybe it came from living and dealing with two hotheads, or maybe he was just born to smooth out their rough edges, but no matter what, Styx was eternally grateful.

The threesome thing certainly wasn't conventional and wouldn't work for everyone, but for the past year, it had run like they'd always been together. Styx never did get his memory back fully, and he'd stopped worrying about it. Not having to look over his shoulder all the time did that to a man.

"Fine—we'll bring Jace." Law snorted at Styx's backtracking and mouthed *whipped*, and Styx bristled but pulled out his phone. He owed Clint everything—his life, the two men who shared his heart and his bed. There was nothing he wouldn't do for Clint. Nothing.

"Tanner's still OUTCONUS himself, and Damon's working that job for us in California—I don't want to pull him off that," Styx said as the phone rang, and the other men nodded.

"You're going to have to give Damon that choice," Law told him as Jace answered with a quick, "Hey."

Without hesitation, Styx said, "He's MIA."

"I knew it. I'm going in."

"By yourself? I don't think so," Styx told him. "We'll all go with you."

"And the CIA's going to be happy about that?" Jace asked.

"I don't worry about what makes the CIA happy anymore," Styx said. "Right now, I'm most concerned with Clint's happiness, and I know that revolves around you."

"It might not anymore, but that doesn't mean I won't do anything I can to save him," Jace said. "When are we leaving?"

Jace was packed and at the airport before any of them. He

boarded the private plane Styx had chartered for them after checking in with the pilot, who explained that he was former Navy.

He tried to settle in for the long flight, but his nervous energy was buzzing through him. He dialed Clint's special number again and left a message with the service, and because he had no idea if Clint was able to access his phone or if someone else was, he simply said, "It's going to be like the first night we got together."

Translation: *I'm coming to save your ass.*

He clicked the phone off as the first of three men boarded.

"Hey, Jace, I'm Styx," the tall, almost white-blond-haired man said. He turned and introduced Law and Paulo. "Law's former Delta, and Paulo was a detective, and you know my deal."

Jace shook the hands of the men he'd heard about many times before, wondered if he'd get the chance to be in a long-term relationship like them.

Except he had been. And now things were fucked beyond repair. If they hadn't fought, maybe Clint wouldn't have taken the job.

"Guilt isn't a good look on anyone," Styx told him.

"Trust him, he's been there," Law added, but he smiled when he said it.

"I didn't say anything."

"Didn't have to," Styx said. "It's written all over your goddamned face. And here I thought SEALs were supposed to be emotionless."

"Ignore both of them," Paulo told him, pushing past the two men to sit close to Jace. He wore jeans and a button-down shirt that was half opened to reveal a black tee underneath, and he shoved a big cammo bag down under one of the seats. He looked cool and collected, and Jace supposed he'd have to be to put up with the two other alphas.

I just need to find him. Whatever else happens from there, it doesn't matter. Jace told himself that, over and over like he was making some kind of pact with the universe.

Let him be okay and I'll let him go, won't bother him anymore.

"Get him to relax and focus," Styx told Paulo, pointing to Jace. "He's too tightly wound to trust."

"Yeah, look who's talking," Paulo muttered. "Get out of here."

Styx listened, he and Law moving toward the front of the plane, leaving the two younger men to talk.

"He's right, you know," Paulo started. "I know it sucks to have to lay your life out to a complete stranger, but Clint's talked about you a lot. I remember hearing about you when you first met."

"Really?"

"He was all kinds of turned around," Paulo said.

"He doesn't trust me. I guess I can't blame him. At first, I hoped it was like when Tomcat had to die and he just needed time before he could make calls. But no matter how pissed he was at me, he'd never do that again—let me think he was dead if it was part of a mission. It's why he gave me the number."

"Mind if I ask what happened?" Paulo asked.

Jace shrugged like it was no big deal, but he had a strange feeling Paulo could see right through him. "I lied to him about why I was hanging out with the Killers."

He told Paulo the whole story, well aware they were all listening. "Kenny's an idiot, but he's the only family I've got."

"Does Kenny know what you're doing for him?" Styx called.

"No specifics. I just told him to shut up and pretend he was happy," Jace said.

"Good."

"The thing with Clint sounds like an argument that would've been solved if Clint hadn't gone MIA," Paulo mused.

"I'm not so sure, but that can't stop me from going to find him."

Chapter Thirty-Two

The thing that kept him going was the knowledge that Jace wouldn't let him die. Clint didn't know how he knew it, why he was so sure after he'd treated the boy like hell, but he knew.

All he had to do was wait. Shackled inside the old warehouse, beaten and left to die, he hadn't. But they'd come back to check, and soon.

God, what a clusterfuck.

He turned, his head pounding, his vision blinded by a swollen shut eye and blood in the other. He checked that he could still feel his feet for the millionth time, and that reassured him somewhat.

He'd been sold out—and he knew by whom.

Sometimes the people you let into your life could be trusted, like Jace, and sometimes they couldn't, like his current employer—Clint had certainly been worried about the wrong damned person. And he'd kill him with his bare hands if he could fucking get free from this place.

Things had gone fine at the start—the first week of the op, when he'd been working as the enforcer for hire for the Iraqi businessman who was really dealing arms, went smoothly, maybe too much so. Now he knew that he'd been sold out on a routine job bringing the man into Afghanistan for a top-secret government meeting.

After surviving two-plus years with one of the most dangerous MC clubs around, he would be damned if he was going to die at the hands of wannabe terrorists. All he had to do was believe that Jace was coming for him. If nothing else, this time he was sure Jace would run to him, not away.

"Look for his last known locale," Styx said as Jace tore through the hotel room looking for anything that might possibly help them discover that.

Finally, he found the matchbook tucked into the mattress. An old spy trick, Clint once told him; something passed down from his father to him.

They'd been discussing how they'd find each other if no one else could. What clues they could leave. And while Jace had never settled on a good method for himself, Clint insisted he adopt this one.

Now, as he stared at the matchbook and the writing inside with the coordinates of Clint's last meeting place, he swallowed hard as he realized that despite Clint's harsh words, he had always believed Jace would be there.

He didn't know where their relationship would go from here, but he did know he could save him.

"I know where he is," Jace said.

He'd been here on a mission recently, within the past year, and the place hadn't changed much, beyond getting more and more violent. Now, as he plugged the coordinates into the GPS just to be sure, he said, "There's a series of abandoned warehouses on the north side of the city—we raided them and found bodies there. We never knew who they were, because the CIA swooped in and took over the case and never contacted us about it again."

242

"Sounds like the agency," Styx agreed.

"What are we waiting for?" Paulo asked impatiently. He was out the door with Jace close behind, Styx on their tail. And yeah, Jace agreed with that impatience, especially because he'd gotten a call hours earlier that he'd be needed within the next several days, which meant if he wasn't back to base before then, he'd be considered AWOL.

Jace guided Law through the dangerous streets while Styx covered them with a waiting gun.

"Gotta get him out before night," Law muttered. None of the streetlights worked. Good for them—better for the criminals.

"We will," Jace said. "We're close. Two more miles."

There were over twenty-five buildings to search. Clint hadn't been that specific, which was smart, although Jace was cursing him now for not giving a little more of a goddamned hint.

"Jace, you're with me—Law, with Paulo," Styx said. It was a risk leaving the car alone, but they needed to cover the space fast. And heavily armed, which they were.

Jace and Styx covered four buildings in the span of half an hour, and they'd found nothing. Same for Law and Paulo, according to their most recent check-in, and Jace tried to shove down his mounting frustration, because that would get them nowhere. He forced himself to remain calm, to forget how damned personal this was, because that's when mistakes were made. And he stayed goddamned professional through another empty building and three quarters of the way through another before something caught his attention.

At first, he thought it might simply be the wind—but something told him to just stop and wait. When he did, hope began to take root again.

Styx was moving ahead, in the opposite direction from the

noise, but Jace tugged at him, told him, "Wait."

Styx did, and for a long moment, they just listened, both men barely breathing in hopes of catching a slight noise. A small groan along with the pull of a chain across the floor came from the north side of the building. "That's got to be him."

"Let's move cautiously," Styx told him, but Jace was beyond listening, beyond caution.

He sped into the room and found Clint on the floor, chained to an old metal radiator. There was blood everywhere, but Clint was alive. Bruised. Battered. But alive. And pissed.

"Hurry," he rasped as Jace struggled with the locks on the chains.

"The tied man isn't usually the one giving orders," Jace muttered as he worked.

"Saved by the Navy...I'll never hear the end of it," Clint groaned.

"Never," Jace told him, right before Clint passed out.

"Better this way," Styx told him, then called to Law and Paulo.

"Tell them to bring a board," Jace told him. "He's moving his legs, but still."

Styx nodded and they waited a tense few minutes until Paulo joined them with the board, saying, "Law's waiting in the car." Paulo helped Jace slide the board under Clint.

As much as Jace wanted to be the one to carry Clint out in his arms, he knew it wasn't for the best. He stared down at the bruised face, thought about how long Clint had been here. Thanked God and everything else that the man had fought, that Jace had listened to his instincts, that he'd hopefully gotten here in time.

And then he prepared for the longest ride of his life—the

one to the military hospital. They were in some dangerous territory, and bullets rang out even as they closed the door and the car sprang away from the curb, with Law doing some serious driving.

Styx and Paulo had their weapons out, and Styx was firing out the window. Clint kept fading in and out of consciousness but he didn't say anything, just watched Jace, and Jace didn't know what the hell to say to him.

I love you. Forgive me. Don't fucking leave me again.

But he'd be damned if he could get any of the words out. Instead, he held Clint's hand the entire way to the hospital, only letting go when the doctors put him on a stretcher and wheeled him back into an exam room.

"He's going to be okay," Styx told him roughly, and Jace nodded numbly.

"Just don't let him be alone," he heard himself say, and the next thing he knew, Styx was leading him back into the exam room, barking orders of his own, and Jace didn't leave Clint's side through any of the treatments that followed.

Clint woke and wished for a long second he hadn't. The pain was helped by the morphine, but he hated being fuzzy and hurt at the same time. He wanted to think clearly and couldn't, and he reached over to rip the IV out of his arm and realized he couldn't.

The thought of being held down—bound—for any reason—made him angry. He turned his head to check out the restraint and saw that it wasn't a rope—it was a hand, attached to a sleeping boy whose head was on the bed. His eyes were closed and there were deep circles under them.

"You've been here for seven days." Styx's voice came from the other side of the bed. "You'd been in the warehouse for two weeks—it's a goddamned miracle you're still alive."

He shifted his head to look at his old partner and friend, who continued, "Jace called me and told me you were missing. He hasn't left your side."

Clint looked over at his hand, twined in Jace's, a tight grip despite the boy's sleep, like he was scared Clint would disappear if given the chance. "Scared the shit out of him again, didn't I?"

Styx nodded. "And now you and I are even. But you still owe Damon and Tanner favors. Jace too, so cut him a break."

Clint rolled his eyes, and just then, Jace stirred.

"I'll leave you guys alone." Styx walked out of the room, and Clint watched Jace go from sleep to instant awareness, courtesy of the SEAL team's relentless training. The fact that Jace had been sleeping that deeply to begin with meant the stress had really gotten to him. That this was really personal.

"Hey," Clint said quietly, afraid Jace would walk out if he said the wrong thing.

"Glad you're okay." Jace stared down at their hands before slowly drawing his away, his fingers sliding from Clint's like sand through an hourglass he couldn't capture or get back.

"Don't leave."

"Clint—" Jace started, stopped for a long moment. "I'm glad I came. But it doesn't change what happened before you left."

"No, it doesn't. I was worried then, and I'm worried now."

"You can't just order me to do stuff outside the bedroom." Jace gave a wry smile, but it didn't reach his eyes.

"You've got to let someone in, dammit. Trust me, even the Lone Ranger needed someone."

"I'm going to fly back separately from all of you. I've got to get back to base ASAP and they're not releasing you for a few days," Jace said as he stood. "You take care of yourself."

"I'm not letting you leave this hospital," Clint told him, and Jace's shoulders went up at the command. "I won't push you away again—not after you got used to me chasing you. That wasn't fair."

"I fucked up too," Jace told him without turning around. "But the fact that you thought I could betray you—"

"I didn't really think that. I was angry. I wanted you to need me."

"I did—I do. Fuck." Jace looked down and finally turned to face Clint.

"Don't make me get off this bed." Clint sat up and winced. "You saved my goddamned life."

"I love you, Clint. But I've got to get back to work."

This time, Jace didn't turn back and Clint let him go, despite his promise not to.

Chapter Thirty-Three

Clint's hospital stay lasted two more weeks, with Styx and Law and Paulo taking turns helping him. He was finally released, and Styx hired a private doctor to fly with him, just in case.

It would be a tough recovery, but with time, he'd heal fully. For now, he felt weak and useless, and he barked at everyone and anyone who tried to help him. The guilt of that overwhelmed him as much as what he'd done to Jace.

"You helped his cousin," Paulo pointed out to him after a month had gone by with no word from Jace.

"Not soon enough. Fuck, I should've guessed Jace would do anything to help his family. Should've known he might do something like working with the Feds. Losing my fucking edge."

"You're losing it where Jace is concerned, period, but that's because you love him. It's hard to see through that, and blaming yourself for everything that happened isn't helping. He loves you—I know it after knowing him for forty-eight hours." Paulo handed him medicine. "Let him come to terms with everything. I know what it's like to fight off what's good for you. I almost ran from these guys."

"I thought he was done running."

"I don't think I'm done yet, some days, and I'm completely in love with both of them." Paulo glanced over at Law and Styx, who huddled over the computer, no doubt planning their next mission. "Go find him."

The look in Paulo's eyes when he said it left Clint little doubt that he truly believed that's what Jace would want.

Clint knew Jace had gotten back from his mission and suspected where he'd find him. His gut led him to the cemetery where he'd found Jace standing over his grave.

The boy was there again, sitting facing Tomcat's grave, but he wasn't crying. No, he was contemplative, like he'd done this before, many times, and Clint wondered if he should walk over, sit next to him.

He decided to wait in Jace's truck instead, noted the surprise on the SEAL's face when he opened the door and found Clint in the backseat where the windows were better tinted.

"Hey."

"Hey." Jace climbed in and started the truck. And then he climbed over the front seat to sit next to Clint in the back, after the heat came on and the doors locked. "Styx told me you've been doing well."

"I figured you'd been keeping tabs on me," Clint said quietly.

"I didn't want to...I couldn't call. Not yet. Not till I figured some stuff out," Jace explained. "I fucked up big-time in all of this. Couldn't figure out my own head. All I knew was that I wanted you from the second I saw you."

Clint prayed there wasn't a *but* at the start of the next sentence. Jace's face flushed a little, the way it always did when they were having sex or Jace was responding to a command or living out a sexual fantasy, and it took everything Clint had not to pull the boy into his lap and kiss the shit—and the hesitation—out of him.

"Don't let me go, Jace," he said finally.

"I won't." Jace's eyes met his. "I just got back this morning. You were going to be my next stop."

"Why come here?"

"Tomcat was the one who first made me realize I was capable of living—of trusting—even if I didn't realize it myself for a lot longer. I thought I owed it to him to tell him that." Jace shrugged. "Probably seems weird."

"Nah—I owe Tomcat a lot." This time he did pull the boy in close, and to his relief, there was no resistance. "You look tired."

"And you look worse." Jace nuzzled him. "I'm fine. Been rough with Kenny, but then WITSEC stepped in and took over. You wouldn't know anything about that, right?"

"Want me to pretend to be innocent?"

"Has that ever worked?" Jace asked, and Clint grinned in response.

"I made some calls about Kenny. Got the Feds moving."

"I should've known better than to trust them."

"You were trying to help someone you love. That doesn't always equal rational decisions," Clint pointed out.

"Yeah, well, I saved your ass by being irrational."

"And I hope you never let me forget it."

Jace laced a hand with his. "I know it was a pain to deal with, so thank you for making sure he's safe."

"And you?"

"They got it when I told them if I stayed in, my CO threatened an investigation," Jace said. "Rex really came through. Sawyer explained everything to him—even though I didn't ask him to."

"You're not angry with him, are you?"

"No, he was just helping."

"I know things are set in motion, but watch your back anyway. Most of the Killers got taken down, but they'll come back. They always do."

"Speaking of coming back, what about you?" Jace asked. "I'll understand if you're not ready to leave the job, not with everything that happened."

"I'm not ready to stop black ops completely, but I don't think you are, either. We could work them together, just without the government jobs holding us back."

"With Styx?"

"Yeah, what do you think?"

"You mean we'd actually live in the same zip code for longer than a week at a time?"

Clint touched Jace's cheek, looked into the boy's eyes. "I was thinking better than same zip. Same house."

Jace's eyes lit up. "Really? You'd do that again, even after..."

"Yeah, even after. I understand what you did, Jace. Probably would've done the same thing in your position. So what do you think—make this permanent? Maybe find a brand-new place and start over? I'd never offer if I wasn't sure."

"I wouldn't say yes if I wasn't sure. So yes," Jace told him.

"Good. Now come on over here and rest with me. I'm an old man, remember?"

Jace laughed softly. "Yeah, that's just how I think of you. That old man I need."

"I love that you need me, Jace. I love..." God, the words had threatened to tumble out so easily, and once he'd realized it, he'd dialed it back.

"I know," was all Jace murmured. "You don't have to say it

251

now. You don't ever have to. When I finally looked at your actions, the way you always came to me, even when I didn't think I could handle us...well, they speak much louder than the words you can't get out."

This kid, this man, melted him. Every. Single. Time. "I love you, Jace."

His voice was gruff, barely recognizable to his own ears...but Jace smiled. Flushed a little. And Clint knew he'd done the right thing.

He cradled Jace against him, kissed him fiercely. Pulled him closer—he finally knew he'd never be happy without this boy.

Never.

Jace practically climbed him. Wrapped around him like he'd finally realized the same thing, murmuring, "I love you," into his ear. And they were naked and fucking right in the damned truck, because that was how they relayed their most intense feelings to each other. This time was no exception.

About the Author

SE Jakes lives in New York where she's currently at work writing her next book. She feels that doing what you love keeps you young and that writing about people falling in love is probably the best damned job in the entire world. You can find out more information about SE's newest books at sejakes.blogspot.com and facebook.com/sejakes.

To get to "Love Me Tender", they'll have to shake things up.

Graceland
© 2012 Ally Blue

Kevin Fraser has a good life—a good job, good friends and a nursing degree within his grasp. There's not a lot of excitement to be found in Asheville, but so what? He doesn't need excitement. Or love, for that matter. Until a big man with an Elvis fixation and the voice to match shows up in his ER and changes his point of view.

A diabetes diagnosis isn't the end of the world, just one more problem Owen Hicks doesn't need. It hasn't been easy finding his place in the Cherokee tribe, his family and the world at large since he came out. On top of that, learning to manage the disease that killed his mother is a daunting challenge. He counts himself lucky that the nursing student he befriended in the hospital is willing and able to help.

As their fast friendship deepens into something both of them want—yet fear—pressures from without and within stretch their bond to the breaking point. The only way to find the strength to love each other is to find the courage to let go...and hope love is strong enough to bring them together again.

Warning: This book contains medical drama, relationship drama, sex, silliness and a Cherokee Elvis. Sorry, no fried banana sandwiches. Thank ya very much.

Available now in ebook and print from Samhain Publishing.

SAMHAIN
PUBLISHING

www.samhainpublishing.com

Green for the planet.
Great for your wallet.

SAMHAIN
PUBLISHING

It's all about the story...

Romance

HORROR

Retro
ROMANCE

www.samhainpublishing.com

CPSIA information can be obtained at www.ICGtesting.com
Printed in the USA
LVOW07s1018070916

503581LV00005B/249/P